5.25

Trail Through Danger

WILLIAM O. STEELE

Trail Through Danger

Illustrated by Charles Beck

HARCOURT, BRACE & WORLD, INC. NEW YORK

For JEAN MAC RAE,
BETTY STAFFORD, *and*
QUINTARD STEELE
from the top of my head
and the bottom of my heart

Trail Through Danger

One

"How come they don't get on back here?" Ela-phelet Birdwell asked himself. "They been gone long enough to find forty-leven trails by now."

It wasn't right for them to take off and leave an eleven-year-old boy all alone with the old man and the loaded pack horses while they tramped through the woods hunting a way down off this mountaintop.

Somebody should have stayed to keep him company, one of the hunters with his rifle. This was Injun country, if it was anybody's. Whoever the redskins found here, they weren't going to feel kindly toward.

He knew he was addled to worry about Indians. He looked around at the horses. They were quiet, and they would know if the savages were about. Yet somehow a body couldn't help feeling uneasy, left here so long with nothing but a butcher knife to fight with.

Mr. Brown muttered fretfully, and Lafe got up and went over to him. The old man lay on a pile of leaves and moss, and even in his sleep he clutched his rifle. A white rag was tied around the end of the barrel. At least, it had started out white, but it was pretty grimy now. Soon somebody was going to have to wash it and freshen it up a mite. That rag was mighty important, for old Mr. Brown was well-nigh blind. He could see things moving about, but he couldn't tell a man from a tree if both were standing still. He had that white rag tied on his gun as a kind of front sight. He could line the rag up with whatever he saw moving. And that's how he meant to kill a buffalo.

"Doty in the head," muttered Lafe. An old codger like that should never have come out on a hunt like this. He ought to be setting home by the hearthside instead of out here in the woods, getting in everybody's way and burdening folks. Especially Lafe.

Mr. Gibbs shouldn't have let the old hunter come along, Lafe thought. But no sooner had Mr. Gibbs started looking around for somebody willing to go west of the Caroliny Mountains hunting with him than Mr. Brown turned up, seeking to be taken along. He had it in his mind to shoot a buffalo, just one more buffalo before he died.

At first Mr. Gibbs had said no. But Mr. Brown had begged and cried and taken on terribly. He said Mr. Gibbs would never rest easy in his grave knowing he'd denied an old man his last wish. Mr. Gibbs seemed willing to run that risk. Finally Mr. Brown said he'd bring his cousin to help him, and he offered Mr. Gibbs a sum of money to take them along. Money was a thing Mr. Gibbs couldn't say no to.

Lafe grimaced. That somebody Mr. Brown had brought with him was Tully Brown. Lafe couldn't abide the man. Tully was as keen a shot as any of the hunters and could get along in the woods just fine.

But when it came to looking out for Old Man Brown, he was always somewhere else.

So the old hunter was one more thing that fell to Lafe's lot, like tending the horses, fetching the wood and water, and doing most of the cooking. He had expected to work, for he had hired himself out to Mr. Gibbs, and his master knew how to get his money's worth out of a body. But there were a lot of times when Lafe wondered how come he was the one to nurse the old man up and down the trail.

Now he leaned down and started to wake up Mr. Brown. Any company was better than none. Then he changed his mind. The old feller looked to be enjoying his rest. Likely he was tired. He'd walked every step of the way here from Carolina, holding on to the horses and toting his rifle.

The boy sat down again. It was a funny thing how just waiting around was so tarnal hard on a body. There were things he didn't much care about doing, like hoeing corn in the hot sun or picking berries for his ma, at least not by his lonesome. But right now he'd give his right big toe to be doing either of them. Anything at all, instead of just sitting here with his back to a tree while the gnats chewed his face to sawdust and the minutes oozed by and darkness slipped up around him.

He took a whetstone from inside his shirt and began to sharpen his knife. It was already honed down to a fine edge, but he had to do something. He felt a heap better, too, with the knife right there in his hand. There wasn't any use telling himself he wasn't scared, sitting here all these hours up on this mountaintop where no white men had ever been before.

He didn't like these woods. There was something about them mighty different from those back home. The trees were big old trees with trunks so large around you wouldn't believe it, but they weren't tall. One of the men said it was the wind kept them stunted and warped-branched like that, and Lafe reckoned it was.

But it wasn't just the trees. It was something about the whole place. It seemed like everything was so old, old and moss covered. Lafe figured these must be the hills that folks said something was as old as. It was a kind of secret place; the trails seemed to close up behind you like water, like the woods made certain that even if you pushed your way in, you'd never find your way back out. Step off the path, and you could feel the strangeness rise up all around you. Everything was different from what it had looked before. The green gloom under the twisted branches pressed down on you. It was frightening.

Lafe looked over his shoulder. He'd noticed before that whenever he was alone, he felt all the time like somebody was close by, staring at him. It gave him the creepy-crawlies up his spine. He wished to goodness one of the others would hurry back.

"How come they don't come back?" he asked aloud. "How come one of 'em ain't remembered *me* sitting here waiting?"

Out of the corner of his eye he made sure he saw somebody slipping toward him. He whirled his head, and fear racketed around inside him. Nothing moved where he looked, but he wouldn't say there was nobody around, for there was.

The woods were filled with wavering shapes, some with topknots of feathers, others carrying tomahawks. It was the Cherokees. They were coming straightway to get him. He knew they were. And they wouldn't care what they did to him for being on their land. He could cry and say it was Aquilla Gibbs's fault, but it wouldn't matter. They'd take his very own knife, sharp as the wind, and use it to slip off his skin and scalp. They'd . . .

Something touched him on the shoulder. He jumped a foot in the air, still sitting, and screamed his head off. Only he was so scared that not a sound came out of his throat.

It was just one of the horses. It'd come up so slow and easy, Lafe hadn't heard a sound. It could have been an Injun. Yet it hadn't been. Lafe picked up the knife that had slipped from his fingers and gave a shaky laugh.

"You scared me for a fact," he told the horse, putting a hand on its warm neck. A beast could be a mighty comforting and friendly thing. He stroked the horse and talked to it softly.

Then all of a sudden he heard voices, and here came Mr. Gibbs and Tully. He didn't care a twang for either one, but now, after his long wait, he felt almost friendly toward them.

"You find a trail?" he called out.

They were walking quickly, almost running, and they didn't answer. They began gathering up the gear as soon as they hit the camp, even Tully. It made Lafe wonder.

"They—they ain't Injuns around, is they?" he asked.

Mr. Gibbs gave him a look. He didn't like his hired help asking questions; it wasn't their place. "Wake the old man," he ordered. "We got to get off this mountain and find a good camp before dark. Don't stand there. Git!"

Lafe wondered where the other two hunters were. Well, he knew better than to ask. They weren't going to wait for them, that was certain. When Mr. Gibbs called out his orders, that was that. He would never waste time nor moccasin leather hunting the others. They toed in to him and his doings, or else.

Lafe went and squatted by Mr. Brown. "Old Man," he called. He reckoned it was disrespectful to call him that, but all the others did, and he'd got in the habit of it. "Old Man, git up. We're moving on." He shook the skinny arm lying across the rifle.

Mr. Brown sat up. "You leave me be," he said. "I ain't one of them no-good, trifling North Mountain Browns. I'm a Stone Church Brown, and we ain't even kin. You ain't got no call to go pushing me around."

Lafe grinned. It always took the old feller a while to come out of his dreams.

"Come along. Wake up now," he told him. "You're out looking for buffalo. Recollect?"

The old hunter rubbed his face and looked around. Then he got to his feet, pretty spry for all his years.

Tully and Mr. Gibbs had most nigh got the gear loaded up. Lafe scowled at Tully's load. It was all whopsided and unlikely looking. It'd slide off the horse on the way down, sure as shooting, and Lafe would be the one to repack it.

Lafe led the old man over to one of the pack horses and guided his hand to a pack thong. "Hang on tight now," he said. "I ain't going to be beside you. I got to lead, I reckon."

In his heart he couldn't see why Tully couldn't lead the pack horses. One of these three was his. But Tully didn't like to do anything that was steady. Even walking, he'd go sometimes fast, sometimes slow, just to change things up a little, or maybe to spite folks. Lafe wasn't sure which. Tully could be precious mean.

They went in single file. First Mr. Gibbs, leading

19

his own three pack horses, then Lafe with the other three and Mr. Brown. Tully came last of all, looking like he owned the whole lot of them. Lafe hoped he'd step in a hole over his head. They could just cover him up and go on off and leave him there.

They scared up a raincrow, and it hollered out. In here under the trees, the bird sounded loud as thunder, and the last "kow" echoed off the trunks. It was kind of weird, but Lafe wished it would call again. He liked raincrows. He could remember them hollering all around his home in the valley of Virginia on summer days.

He glanced up to see the bird swoop overhead, slim silver body and long, spotted tail. Who could tell, this very same bird might have flown down here from his homeplace. He stiffened. He'd promised himself he wasn't going to think about his home.

Home had got so it seemed almost as strange as these woods. It just didn't make sense that a little while back he'd had a home and a ma and pa like anybody else. At that time he had lived in a cabin with a sister and a brother, and they kept a cow and a horse and hens.

It was all like that one day, and the very next day

it was gone. Oh, all those things were still *there*. You could still lay your hand on the cabin door and holler out your brother's name and eat the hens' eggs. But something that had happened made it all so different, he might as well have been a total stranger in that cabin. He might as well have been eating woodchips and river mud and been called by another name.

He quit thinking about it.

They went along and along. The trees thinned, and looking up, Lafe saw that it was not so late in the day as he'd figured it to be. That was one thing about deep forest; it could fool you every time.

Still, when they came out on the edge of the mountain where the trail started down, it was late enough. The sun was sliding into a layer of clouds banked along the western sky.

"Yonder," Mr. Gibbs said softly. Lafe hurried up to stand beside him.

The wide, rolling green valley lay beneath them, stretching farther than a body could see. It wasn't all woods. Even in the dimming light, Lafe could make out savannas and canebrakes and the winding traces of rivers and creeks.

"Best hunting land in the whole wide world," Mr.

Gibbs went on. He was so happy that he all but danced a jig there on the rocky ledge. Lafe could tell he was already counting up all the money he was going to make from this hunting journey. "Best in the whole world!"

"By the end of August we'll have all the skins we can carry back," Tully said. He licked his lips.

"The Lord willing," Mr. Gibbs added.

Somebody hollered from below. It was Noah Finny. He'd been part way down the mountainside, checking the trail. Now he'd come back to meet them, but he didn't come all the way to the top. He stood about ten feet down the path waiting for them. Then a funny thing happened, something Lafe didn't remember seeing in all his life before.

The world turned red—trees, trail, everything. The sky blazed deep gold-crimson, and the air was like blood and water. Lafe looked down at his brown hands, and even they were dyed deep red.

"It looks like the end of the world," Tully spoke out.

Noah took the rest of that trail in a single leap. His eyes were like eggs, they were so big and white in his face. "It's the end of the world!" he bawled. "The end of the world!"

Mr. Gibbs brushed by Noah and eased cautiously down the steep path with his horses. Tully stood there and gave one of his sly grins, saying nothing. The color deepened.

"It was just those clouds," Lafe told himself, "just the sun through those banked clouds. Nothing more. It wasn't a sign from heaven or a warning or anything." Noah must think fire and brimstone were going to rain down, as scared as he acted. Noah's trouble was dim-wittedness. He was never mean; he just wasn't too smart. He thought the best and all of Tully Brown and repeated whatever Tully said as though it were the gospel truth.

Noah moaned a little, and his head rolled around on his shoulders. Then he ran after Mr. Gibbs. Lafe pulled on his lead rope and began the slow descent. Noah was a ninny. It was just a real red sunset, the light through the clouds.

But he couldn't help shivering. It seemed somehow a bad beginning for them, a dark, unlucky way to start a hunt in an empty, unfriendly land.

Still, it was too late for him to turn back. There wasn't anything to do but go on into this country that was so strange, there wasn't a name put to any part of it.

Two

The trail down was steep and rough, but Lafe and the others hurried as best they could in the fading light. Before black dark they found a place to camp close to a creek.

Lafe reckoned he was going to appreciate his bed this night. It wasn't just that he was so tired; it was mostly he was so glad to be off that mountaintop. He glanced up. The rock cliffs still gleamed in the last light, white streaks across the dark hump of the mountain. It was kind of ghostly. He didn't know why it had seemed so queer and unfriendly up there, but it had. Now down here, it was different.

Lightning bugs flared up over the meadow. The shoals in the creek made a steady ruffling noise, like birds' wings. Once a bullfrog grunted. The air was hot and summer-sweet with the smell of grass and leaves.

In the dark Lafe set to work to untie the leather pack lines, fumbling at the knots and wishing for a light. Tully went off muttering something about hearing turkeys hollering as they settled down in their night's roost.

Lafe grinned a little to himself. He knew what kind of turkey Tully Brown had heard, the kind with nine wings, a round pulley bone, and three heads. It was the same kind he heard most every candlelight when there was work to do.

He shrugged. If Mr. Gibbs and Noah didn't care, he didn't give a hoot either. Tully wouldn't stoop to pick up firewood anyway. Lafe eased a pack to the ground.

"Never mind that," Mr. Gibbs stopped him. "Me and Noah'll do that. You fetch some wood and get a fire going."

It was easier finding dried cane than untying knots, and in a moment or two Lafe had as much as he could carry. On the way back up the bank, he stumbled on a half-rotted pine branch. He snatched that, too. He dumped his load to the ground and took out his flint and steel and a little wad of tow. A spark flew into the tow and it smoldered. He blew on it gently.

Tiny flames crept over the cloth, and he fed cane leaves and pine needles into it. Mr. Gibbs moved off toward the creek with the unloaded pack horses, singing a hymn the way he always did, going up when he ought to go down and down when he ought to be up, and then rasping along on the middle parts. Lafe's mother used to sing that hymn, he remembered. Not the way Mr. Gibbs sang it. Like he was dying of a painful case of the inside cobbles was how it sounded to Lafe.

Just the other day Rice McCay had made Lafe laugh by telling how he was standing right beside Mr. Gibbs when he started to sing one of his hymns.

27

At the first bellow, Rice said, he was blown clean out of sight over the treetops.

With pieces of the pine branch and sticks of cane, Lafe fed the blaze and moved back from the heat. He wished he hadn't thought about his mother. During the day he wasn't bothered. If he remembered her, it didn't seem to matter so much. But at night— sometimes he reckoned he couldn't bear it. Sometimes he got so mad and so sorrowful that it had all happened, he just knew his ribs would fly open and let his insides spill out.

He put on the last of the pine, and the fire sprang up. Down at the creek another fire blazed in the water. Lafe could hear the hobbled horses crunching the cane. One of them lifted its head, and the firelight caught its eye and made it gleam.

Noah came up with a pine torch and thrust it into the flames. "Let's us go fire-hunting," he said to Mr. Gibbs. "I crave fresh meat the worst way."

Mr. Gibbs considered. "Without a boat?" he asked. "It ain't easy, wading. Too much noise."

"Fresh meat taste mighty good," urged Noah.

"Well, you never spoke a truer word than that,"

admitted Mr. Gibbs. " 'Twon't hurt to try. I'll fetch my rifle, and you can hold the torch."

On their way to the creek, they passed Lafe gathering more cane. "Git that pot ready, boy," boasted Noah. "We aim to bring back meat a-plenty."

Lafe didn't answer. He just went on back to the fire with his armload. He made note of a dead tree and figured it might be worth the work to chop it down. It might be easier than trying to find a night's firewood by the flickering light.

Old Mr. Brown was crouching by the blaze. He was shaking like he had the ague. "You all right?" asked Lafe anxiously.

The old man looked up and grinned a little. "I'm tired, is all," he answered. "We come down that trail like a runaway hoopsnake. Lemme get warm and I'll be fine."

"Something to eat would help him, too," Lafe thought. The old man was bound to be hungry. The last thing any of them had eaten was breakfast way back up on the mountain. He shouldered the ax and went over to the dead tree. It was almost too doty. Four strokes and it came crashing down.

He quickly split it into lengths. Gathering up some of the wood, he headed back for the camp. Tully was there, squatting off by himself. He was in the shadows, and he was eating something, Lafe could tell, chewing away for dear life and brushing his mouth with the back of his hand.

Lafe gave him a scornful look and went for more wood. He knew Tully had something put by, dried meat and corn. He'd seen him hiding things more than once. He knew Tully had been making ready against a night like this, when they were out of meat and chances of getting fresh game were scarce.

The fire was leaping bright and friendly now. Lafe fetched a pot of water. They could have hot mush if they didn't have anything else. He hoped against hope Mr. Gibbs would come in toting some meat. And he hoped by the time it happened, Tully would have his craw full of dried corn and not be able to eat a collop.

"Fire feels fine, don't it?" quavered Mr. Brown.

Lafe was relieved to see how much better he looked now. "My pa always said a fire was the next best thing to a dog for making a body feel at home, no matter where he was at," the boy said.

"Dogs! Fires!" Tully spoke up in his hatefulest voice. "They ain't neither one much use out in the woods, not for hunting nor Injun-killing, either one. A gun's what counts. I reckon your pap wasn't much of an Injun fighter, now was he?"

Lafe's heart slowed in his chest, and his blood went in a little cold trickle of fear and anger. How come Tully never failed to make a slight on his pa? What did he suspicion?

Lafe didn't dare look around at him. "He done his share while he was alive," he answered gruffly at last.

Then he set to work fixing stones for the pot of water to rest on. There wasn't any use him worrying over Tully Brown. Tully didn't know a thing. Mr. Gibbs didn't know, even. Lafe had told Mr. Gibbs a flat lie and said his ma and pa were dead, and Mr. Gibbs hadn't questioned it.

There were some folks living in Caroliny who knew the truth about him. Some near his Uncle George's farm at Salisbury. They knew all right. To this day Lafe didn't know how they'd found out, for Salisbury was a long piece from his old home in Virginia. The news couldn't have traveled so far. But once the neighbors began looking sort of slaunchways at Uncle George and his barn and his fields—well, Lafe could see how it was.

Once again his troubles had caught up with him, and he'd had to move on to get away from them. When he'd heard Aquilla Gibbs was looking for a likely lad to go with him on this hunt, he'd walked a whole day, mighty fast, to take the job.

Uncle George had seen him go without much more than a wave of the hand. Lafe could understand why. After all, he wasn't, for a fact, any real kin of George Hastings. Uncle George was the uncle of Lafe's sister Miriam's husband. And when Lafe had turned up one day, Uncle George had been glad enough to see him, an able-bodied, hard-working, quiet boy. He'd said as much. But later when folks started whispering about Lafe and his family, Uncle George had soured on his visitor.

So here Lafe was, out in the middle of the wilderness, and nobody here knew a thing about him. Tully couldn't have found out anything. He was just natural-born mean and knew every kind of hateful trick and how to squeeze out of people whatever thing bothered them. Well, Lafe didn't reckon he'd let *this* be squeezed out of him. Never!

Somebody was coming. It sort of scared Lafe for a minute to hear the bushes rustling. He could only think that Indians had seen the fire, and how few there were in the hunting party, and aimed to walk in and take over. But it was Rice McCay who slipped out of the shadows with a deerskin over his shoulder. He dropped it by the fire, and it fell open so Lafe could see the chunks of dark meat.

The collops were a welcome sight. Yet he'd have been glad to see Rice without any meat. "I made sure we'd lost you for good," he said.

"It's a mite hard to lose me, for a fact," Rice answered. "Now you folks, that's different. I can lose you without hardly any trouble. But me—I don't get lost."

Lafe grinned and took out his knife and began to cut up some of the bigger pieces of deer meat into the pot. After a minute, Rice squatted to help him. Lafe wished it was just the two of them out here hunting all by themselves—just him and Rice, without Noah's foolishness or Mr. Gibbs's fretting or Tully's meanness.

Rice went and cut some cane slivers. When he came back, he handed one to Tully. "Here," he said mildly, "you can roast some meat for the old man."

Tully gave him a look, but he took the stalk of cane. Lafe ducked his head so Tully couldn't see him grinning. Rice was the only one who could get the better of Tully.

Tully might be a little scared of the younger man, Lafe figured. Rice was big and strong, stronger than Tully, but Lafe had never seen him act uppity or lose his temper. He wasn't likely to take advantage of Tully.

When some of the collops were roasted, they ate. Tully ate as much as the rest, in spite of his earlier meal of dried meat and corn.

"How'd you get this here deer?" he asked Rice.

"Shot it," answered Rice briefly. Tully flushed and looked put out.

"I know that," he said. "But I didn't see no deer sign on that mountain. I looked good."

"Well, this'un was there," said Rice. And he didn't say any more.

Rice wasn't much for talking ever. He was friendly as could be, quick to be helpful or give a cheerful

34

word to Lafe or Old Man Brown when the going was hard. But he stayed away from the others a lot, off hunting by himself or just walking ahead, kind of like a scout. When he was with them, he hardly ever had anything to say about himself or what he had done or how he'd done it. And even if he did talk about himself, Lafe always got the feeling he was talking mighty careful so as not to tell anything that was much account.

"Yonder comes Gibbs," said Mr. Brown suddenly. He had a keen pair of ears to make up for not having much in the way of eyes, and he'd heard the two fire-hunters returning before any of the other three did.

Noah and Mr. Gibbs were empty-handed, and they were mortal glad for that deer of Rice's, Lafe could tell.

"We ain't seen no game," said Mr. Gibbs, frowning. "I hope it ain't going to be this way the whole time. I've heared tell of folks coming into a hunting ground like this, where game is thick as fleas most times, and them not being able to lay a hand on so much as a squirrel. Everything just up and took off afore they got there."

35

"Rice here, he'll find it for you," said Tully. "He's got a nose for red blood."

Rice lifted his head quickly and stared at Tully. "It'd be a mighty poor hunter couldn't find game, one way or another," he said finally. He went over to his pack and took out a gourd, then helped himself to stew from the pot.

Tully shrugged and licked his fingers. The old man belched, and a bullfrog answered down at the creek.

Lafe watched Rice, thinking hard. He liked him just a heap. Maybe because he was so young, not much more than eight or nine years older than Lafe. Maybe because he was just a good sort of fellow. And whatever his reasons for keeping himself to himself, it was all right with Lafe. He didn't have it in mind to get too friendly with anybody, either.

But it worried him to think there might be a way for Tully to get at Rice.

"I heard of a man could tell the weather by looking at bloodstains," Noah spoke up. "Only trouble was he was a poor shot. Somebody else had to kill game for him to read the weather signs."

"I can do my own shooting," Mr. Gibbs said. "And

I pray I'll find plenty to shoot pretty soon. I come out here to get enough skins to buy a farm with, and I don't hardly know what I'd do if'n I didn't get 'em."

"Then you sure better dry out that rifle lock," Noah said. "As many times as you went down in them deep creek holes tonight, it'll be wet clean through."

Mr. Gibbs nodded. "I aim to clean it. I got along another in my pack. Away far off from the settlements, it don't pay just to bring one rifle gun."

Tully turned to Lafe. "See what I mean, boy?" he asked harshly. "Ain't no fire or dog can do for you what a gun can do. Reckon your pap didn't know that, did he? Reckon that's how come you're an *orphan* now."

Once again Lafe felt that little chill in his innards, the way Tully sneered out that word "orphan."

All of a sudden Rice spoke up. "I reckon you're an orphan, too, Tully," he said. "Any man and woman had a brat ugly as you be likely killed themselves the same day."

His voice was steady and calm, but it was as full of warning as if he'd raised a loaded rifle to his shoulder.

Lafe stared miserably into the fire. In a minute he got up and fetched his quilt and lay down on it, away from the others. It didn't make him feel any better to have Rice stand up for him. He could fight his own battles. Had to, even with Tully. What's more, he didn't want to think he'd dragged Rice into his troubles.

"I done brought my bad luck with me, for a fact," he thought dismally. If Tully knew the truth, he wouldn't tell it right out; he'd let it seep and slide out in little ways, just the way he'd been doing.

Long after the blaze had died down and the others had gone to sleep, Lafe lay there under the trees with his eyes wide. He could hear Mr. Gibbs's big rough snores and old Mr. Brown's high weird ones that had about scared him to death the first night they were on the trail. But over and beyond those sounds, he could hear the heavy thud of his own heart and some voice inside his head asking over and over, did Tully really know?

Three

It was hot. Even under the trees, the air was thick
with heat. Sweat made Lafe's shirt cling to his shoulder blades. He wiped his face on his sleeve. It might
be he'd have to take his shirt off and go bare naked
before long. If it was this hot with the sun not halfway up the sky, what would it be by noon?

He had already made out this was going to be a

long, tiresome day. They'd got up before daybreak. A chittydiddle had been hollering still. They'd been hurrying along the trail before it was good light. For once they were all together, even Tully and Rice.

Of course, Mr. Gibbs was so eager, sometimes he pulled ahead of the others. He didn't have to bother with the horses, and once or twice he'd got clean out of sight. They could tell he was there, though, by the bellows.

"Oh, I'm headed for a land of pure delight," he bawled.

Lafe grimaced. Was there ever such hymn singing?

"He's headed for good hunting and a heap of skins and the money they'll fetch," exclaimed Tully. "Pounds and pence are the purest delight he can think of."

"Well, that's what he come for," pointed out Rice. "And I don't reckon you plan to go home empty-handed."

Tully grinned. "Not me, I don't," he agreed. "I aim to shoot so many buffalo, there won't hardly be none left for the rest of ye."

"Leave me one, boy," quavered Old Man Brown. "Leave me one."

"And I have it in mind to kill the first one," Tully boasted. "Hey, Noah, I'll lay you a horn of powder I'll kill the first one."

Noah shrugged and smiled a little foolishly. "I ain't laying no wagers," he answered. "I ain't never set eyes on one of the beasts. It might be I'd see the first one and not know it from a gully jumper." He looked uneasy. "I hear tell they ain't the easiest critters to kill. Got to be shot just so. Say some of the bulls is big as a cabin."

"Bigger," Tully told him. "A herd of them big fellers is so all-fired heavy that when they graze a meadow, the land is liable to sink down as much as a foot under 'em."

Noah glanced uncertainly at the others. "Is that right?" he asked. "Is that a fact now?"

"True as I'm walking here," said Rice. "The land sinks down and kinda catches. It don't spring right back up when them buffalo get off it. No siree, it may be a day or even a week, and then it springs up all of a sudden. If you was to be on that meadowland when it happened, you might get throwed up in the air."

Noah looked down and kicked at a stick alongside the path. Mr. Brown spoke up. "I knowed a feller it happened to one time. Pitched him so high in the air, an eagle come flying along and grabbed him. Figured he must be some new kind of bird and fetched him back to its nest to feed the young 'uns."

He cackled softly, "Heeheeheeee," like what he was going to tell was so funny he could hardly wait, he had to laugh ahead of time. "What saved that man was his ears. They was so big and stuck out so far, the little eagles couldn't swaller him! Heeheehee!"

Lafe and Rice laughed, too, but Tully looked solemn as Sunday. "So you be keerful," he warned Noah.

Noah grinned. "That there's all a lie," he announced. "Ain't nobody got ears that big!"

Lafe wondered about Noah. He was foolish, for a fact he was. But Lafe could never make out how much of Tully's tales Noah believed and how much he didn't. Sometimes it seemed like Noah was leading Tully on, as much as Tully was leading him.

"Well, right on, I'll lay a horn of powder I shoot

42

the first buffalo," repeated Tully. Then he and Noah fell to arguing over the price of powder back in Salisbury. Their steps got slower as their words grew louder and louder. Rice and Lafe pulled on ahead of them and, where the trail widened, walked side by side.

Rice didn't say anything, and Lafe didn't mind. He didn't have much to say himself. Whenever he opened up and got to talking a lot, it made him shudder to think about it afterwards, how easy it would have been for something to slip out. Try as he might to forget what his pa had done, he hadn't succeeded. It just seemed to wait right there at the back of his tongue, ready to come busting out anytime. So mostly he tried to keep his mouth shut, especially when the talk turned to Indians or somebody like Noah's cousin, who'd been a trader to the Shawnees and married him a squaw-woman.

All of a sudden Rice turned and asked, "How'd you like to shoot a buffalo?"

"I reckon it would be fine," Lafe answered without thinking because he'd already spent a heap of time wondering if he'd have a chance. He hoped Rice would offer to let him use his rifle. They walked on a way, and Lafe waited for Rice to speak. But the hunter seemed to have forgotten him altogether and just ambled along, staring straight ahead.

Rice's eyes were the bluest things Lafe had ever seen. Maybe it was because his face was so tanned. His skin was the color of an old saddle, and that was the truth. He never wore any kind of a covering on his head, and his hair was bleached almost white. He wore it clubbed in the back and looked for all the world like a blue-eyed, white-haired Indian, Lafe thought.

But there was something more about Rice's eyes than their blueness and the way they were set in his dark skin, something that bothered Lafe a heap. It was this: when you looked right into them, you never saw anything there. They were kind and even friendly, but something closed up sharp and tight in them, like a door between Rice and the rest of the world. If you'd told Lafe a man could do that, he wouldn't have believed it.

It was so, though, for once or twice Lafe had come on Rice when the door was open, when the hunter looked different altogether. But only for a minute.

Then whatever it was slid shut again, and Rice was by himself, back there wherever he was hiding.

Now once again something flickered and deepened in Rice's blue eyes, and he said, "It ain't so great. You'd be surprised how many things in this world ain't as great as you figure when you come to do 'em."

It was a queer thing to say, especially the way Rice said it, like this was a thing that meant a heap to him. Lafe just went on walking. But he reckoned this time Rice was dead wrong. It must be mighty fine to shoot a big beast like that and then own it all—the hide, the great furry head and the horns, and slabs and slabs of meat. It would be a thing to talk about for a long time. It would be . . .

Lafe jerked his shoulder. It wasn't a thing for him to ponder over, anyway. He didn't have a gun. He hadn't come out here to hunt. He had his tasks to do and his money to earn, and that was all. He might as well keep his mind off hunting buffalo.

All day long they followed the trail, under huge beeches and around locust thickets, through cane-brakes and across a hundred creeks. "It ain't so different from Virginny," thought Lafe. "Only they ain't no pines. I ain't seen a pine since we come off the mountain."

There were red cedars in gracious plenty, however. Whenever the trace topped a rise, you could look out and see a dozen knolls looming up out of the rest of the green, dark and somber with cedars. Some of them were twisty, scrawny little fellers, poking up out of cracks in the limestone rocks. Yet some were huge, straight and cone-shaped, big enough to yield piggins and churns for a whole township.

They brought Lafe's father to mind every little bit, and he didn't like it. His pa had always talked about how piggins shouldn't be made of anything but cedar. It was just one of his notions, Lafe reckoned, though he'd heard lots of people say that cedar wood made water sweeter.

His pa had been notional about a-plenty of other things, at least about food and drink. He said it wasn't cleanly to drink out of the same dipper as somebody else, and he wouldn't eat off a wooden trencher but had a pewter plate that Lafe's mother scoured bright every day.

"I reckon he ain't so picky now," Lafe thought,

"a-dipping out of a common pot with the Injuns, eating dog and goodness knows what other trash." He didn't know whether it pleased him or hurt him to think about it.

They came to a creek, and Lafe was so busy thinking, he was in it up to his knees before he knew he was wet. Upstream a beaver slapped the water with its tail. The sound was sharp and clean through the heavy air of the hot afternoon. Mostly there wasn't anything to hear but the whir and tick and buzz of grasshoppers and jarflies.

Rice aimed his gun that way. "Beaver's hard to shoot," he told Lafe. "Hardest thing in the world. They're quick and they're careful."

"I ain't come out here to shoot no beaver," Tully said sourly. "I come to shoot buffalo but don't seem like I'm going to git the chance."

They hadn't seen a trace of one, for a fact. They came on deer sign a-plenty and once bear sign. And turkeys gobbled off in the beech woods, pigeons flocked in the cedars, and rabbits bounded everywhere. "You couldn't starve in this country if you tried," Lafe thought.

Mr. Gibbs urged them to hurry. They were following a buffalo road and were bound to come on the beasts soon. But they didn't, not that day nor the next.

Tully got meaner and meaner. He snarled at everybody. Lafe wished he could let the things Tully said slide off him, the way Rice did. But he couldn't. Let Tully sneer out about how some folks were left so helpless in this world, or let him pretend he had forgotten that Lafe's pa and ma were dead, and Lafe could feel himself crouch like a quail in the weeds with a hawk going over.

The morning of the third day in the valley was the worst of all. Even the pack horses were cross-grained and surly. The heat and the gnats were driving them wild. Rice went on off while the rest of them were squabbling over whether they ought to leave right now or later, with breakfast or without, on the left side of the trail or the right. Lafe couldn't draw breath without Tully or Mr. Gibbs snapping his head off.

It was no better once they were under way. Tully's horse got mired. Mr. Gibbs busted open a wallet of corn. They ranted and raved till Lafe didn't care any more what they said to him or did. The path could

48

open up and swallow them all, including him, and he wouldn't mind.

Then about midmorning, they pushed out of a steaming canebrake onto the bank of a creek. A long sandbar ran out into the water, some kind of little purple flower bloomed thick along one side, and mussel shells lay around showing their rainbow-colored insides. Tully plopped down on the sand with his back against a half-buried log.

"I ain't fixing to move another step," he announced. "I got a stone bruise on my heel big as a egg."

Noah sat down, too, cross-legged, with his rifle on his lap. Lafe was glad for some rest. He splashed water on his face and neck and then waited by the animals. The horses stood quietly, weary from the day's travel.

Mr. Gibbs frowned. "There's licks ahead," he said. "Bound to be buffalo and deer there in their hundreds. We come out here to get game, not to set around dilly-dallying on a creek bank. Get up, Tully, let's be off."

"Come on, Tully," begged Mr. Brown. "I could

just as easy wake up dead tomorrow as not. I aim to get me a shot at a buffalo quick as I can, just in case. Don't keep us here."

"Shut up, Old Man. You whine worse than the gnats. And I'd as soon squash you," Tully snarled. He glanced up at Mr. Gibbs. "And don't order me around. I ain't hired help like the orphan you got."

Mr. Gibbs flushed red and opened his mouth, and just then there was a tremendous splashing upstream. They all turned to look. There was a great bull elk stalking through the shallow water. Lafe gasped. He'd never seen an elk before. It was bigger than he'd figured anything could be, and its antlers spread out from its head like two trees.

They were all startled. Mr. Gibbs just stood there looking with his mouth still open, but Tully started grabbing around for his gun.

"I'll get him! I'll get him!" hollered Noah and tried to jump to his feet and aim at the same time. He stumbled, and his rifle slipped from his hands and struck the ground and went off. The ball ripped into the log where Tully was still sitting.

The report was loud up and down the creek. As

it echoed away, Tully turned and put his finger in the bullet hole beside him.

Lafe grinned. It had missed by a good foot, but he could tell Tully figured himself half dead and was furious about it.

Tully staggered to his feet. He raised his own rifle as if he were going to bring it crashing down on Noah's head. "What the devil you up to, you witless fool?" he bawled. "You trying to kill me? You ain't fit to spit on!"

He lowered his gun and snatched up Noah's and flung it as far as he could. It sailed through a little clump of willows and landed in the creek.

"I never went to, Tully," began Noah in a scared voice. But Tully splashed away across the fording place and never looked back. The old man stumbled along behind him, hardly able to keep up with the pack horse he was frantically clinging to. Mr. Gibbs followed right behind them.

"I never went to do no harm," moaned Noah meekly. "I just aimed to kill a elk."

Lafe had a friendly feeling for Noah, mostly because of the way Tully had jumped and turned pale when the bullet jarred into the log. "I'll help you find your rifle," he offered. "It ain't deep water. We can find it easy."

But finding it took longer than he'd figured. The others were long gone, clean out of hearing and more, before he and Noah found the spot where the gun lay and fetched it up out of the riffles and shook the drops from it. Then they had to catch Noah's horse that had strayed down the branch. All in all, the others had a good start on them.

They crossed to the other bank and pushed in among the cane along the winding path. "Them others had ought to of waited for us," complained Noah. "I kin follow a trail good as the next man. But it don't take but the least little wrong turn to get lost in a brake. Just get a foot off the trace, and there you are inside and can't get out."

"There's their prints, plain as day," said Lafe. "I can follow them. I'll go first."

"Well, then, maybe they done got lost, and we're lost, too," went on Noah. Then he looked puzzled, as though there were something about this that wasn't quite right. "Anyway, it ain't just getting lost. It's Injuns laying in wait, and catamounts and bears and snakes—ever kind of bad thing in a brake like this."

Lafe hurried on. Noah made him jumpy, for a fact, so every hang-on-the-limb hollering, every shike-poke flying over made him want to run for cover. He made sure he was dead a dozen times before they got out of the cane.

Though Lafe kept Noah trotting, it was not till midday that they caught up with the rest of the men. They were standing beside the trail. Rice was with them, and there was an air of excitement that startled Lafe. "Injuns!" he thought. But it wasn't. It was buffalo tracks around a muddy place where the beasts had been wallowing.

"Their bodies get plumb naked in the summer," explained Rice. "Gnats and flies and such nearabout drive 'em wild, so they plaster up good with mud when they can, and I reckon it helps."

Lafe wondered what a buffalo really looked like, all plastered up with mud at the back end, humped and hairy and horned at the front. Just thinking about it made him tingle all over. He was as wild as Tully and Mr. Gibbs to get on. But before he left the wallow, he knelt and ran his finger around the edge of the track. It wasn't much to look at, just like a cow's print, only a heap bigger. But it was a buffalo track. Buffalo! Just saying it over made his breath come quick with excitement. He'd like to shoot one his very own self. Oh, how he'd like to! He jumped to his feet and ran after the others.

They went along the path as fast as they could make it. The trees thinned, and there were more bushes. They were coming to a clearing. Even the horses seemed to push forward as eagerly as the men.

There was a meadowland up ahead, a wide plain, green with tall grass, gently rolling toward the blue distance. And here and there a big dark shape, strange and a little scarifying.

"Buffalo!" gasped Mr. Gibbs, and dropped his line to run forward.

But Tully sprinted ahead of them all. And there rising up out of the grass right in front of him was one of the beasts, a huge, shaggy bull with a wild mane. It was on its knees in the awkward way of the cattle kind, pawing to get up off the ground.

Tully shot, hardly stopping to aim. The bull gave a muffled bellow and rolled over on its side and lay still.

"I done shot me one," yelled Tully. "I done got the first one! I told you I would!"

He ran forward, waving his gun over his head and jumping up in the air every few steps like a skip-jack. When he got to the bull, he didn't stop. He just ran right up on it like it was a little hill and stood there crowing.

Lafe never forgot what happened next, for that old bull wasn't dead. The very next second it was lunging to its feet and standing up. Tully's rifle flew up in the air as he clutched at the hump. And there he went, riding a buffalo bull across the meadow!

Four

Lafe hadn't known a big critter like that could run like a whirlwind. He didn't think he'd ever seen a horse to outrun that bull. It raked its tail straight up in the air and took off like wildfire, in a wide circle through the grass.

There wasn't a sound but the steady clatter of its hoofs and every now and then a high-pitched squeal from Tully. The other five of them stood there gaping like chickens with the pip, so thunderstruck they never moved when the great beast came galloping right at them, turning so close they could hear the weeds slither along its sides.

"What—what is it?" stammered Mr. Brown. He clutched at Lafe's arm with his thin hand, as dry and hot as though he'd been a-bed with the fever.

"It's Tully," Lafe managed to squeak out. "A big ol' bull done run off with him. He got up on it when he figured it was dead, but it weren't, and now it's done run off with him!"

Tully was clinging on for all he was worth. He'd managed to get astride the buffalo and had his hands knotted in its mane. Lafe admired to see how tight he hung on, like the world's biggest cocklebur.

"Show me where it's at," begged the old man. "I'll shoot it. Just show me where it's at."

"Hit's away off now," said Lafe. "Anyhow, you'd kill Tully sure. If you didn't hit him with a ball, the bull would fall on him."

"Here it comes back," cried Rice softly, and it did, racing over the meadow with Tully bouncing on its back like a drop of water on a hot skillet.

"We got to get back," Lafe cautioned the old man.
"It's headed right this way! It's going to run over us!"

"Is it still got Tully?" begged the old man. "Is it
done throwed him?"

"Naw," the boy answered. "He's a-holding on.
Look . . . looky there. The critter's fixing to fall
. . . it's down, it's down on one knee."

As the buffalo swayed and stumbled, Tully flung
himself to the ground.

"He's off!" cried Lafe, shaking Mr. Brown's arm hard. "Tully's done got off. He'll have to run for it now!"

But Tully couldn't seem to find his feet. They could see him good, for the grass was thinner there at the edge, and he was well-nigh digging a hole in the ground trying to get up and run at the same time.

Noah groaned. "He'll git killed," he hollered, and put his hands over his eyes. "He'll git gored sure."

"I seen two men gored," said Mr. Brown. "And one trampled in the dust till we couldn't never find no two parts of him fitted together."

The bull had recovered and wheeled. It was coming right at Tully. Lafe gasped. One hook of one of those horns and Tully'd be ripped wide open. The man was on his feet and racing now, right for a big oak tree standing out a little from the others. "He's going to make it," Lafe cried to Mr. Brown. "Tully's going to swing up in that tree—but he'd better make it quick."

Tully jumped for the limb but missed it clean, and the bull all but touched him. Tully dodged around the trunk. The bull stopped and lowered its head and stomped the dusty ground. Then it began to trot around the tree, and Tully stumbled along, just barely ahead of the beast.

"It's chasing Tully around the tree," Lafe yelped. "It's going a heap faster than he is. It's got him this time, for sure."

He looked around at the others. Noah still had his hands over his eyes and was hopping up and down. Mr. Gibbs was just standing there like he'd been turned to stone. But Rice had the queerest look on his face Lafe had ever seen.

"How come you don't help him?" Lafe burst out. "How come you all don't go shoot at it?"

Tully and the bull were whirling around the tree. It seemed to Lafe those little wicked horns must be touching the man, they were so close. Rice muttered something and stepped forward and then began to run. The buffalo suddenly flung up its head and stopped and then turned and trotted off toward the rest of the herd, as though that was what it had in mind to do all along.

"What happened?" bawled the old man, clutching Lafe.

"It's gone," breathed the boy. He pulled himself loose from Mr. Brown's clutching hand. "It just went

off and left him." But he wasn't watching Tully or
the bull now. He was eying Rice, for Rice had
dropped his rifle and was leaning way over, holding
his belly like he had the colic. So that had been what
ailed Rice. He'd looked so strange because he was
about to bust out laughing. Now he was whooping
fit to split. He sank to his knees, snorting and shaking, and finally he gave up and lay on the ground.
"He looks to be having a fit," Lafe thought. He'd
heard tell of people rolling on the ground, they
laughed so hard, but he'd never seen anybody do
it before.

"Hoo, hoo, hoo!" roared Rice. "Ha, ha heeeee!"

It made Lafe sort of giggle just to hear him. He
began to chuckle. It had been funny, come to think
of it, Tully bouncing along on the bull, and then the
two of them whirling around the tree like they were
partners stepping along to a play-party tune. He
opened his mouth to laugh out, and then he happened to glance at Tully leaning against the tree.
It dried up the laugh in his chest. Even all that way
across the grass, Lafe could feel Tully's look. It was
like pulling your bare face through a bunch of cat-

briers. He wouldn't have thought one man could be as hateful-mean as Tully looked right then.

Lafe wanted to tell Rice to shut up. He went over and laid his hand on his shoulder, but Rice didn't pay him any mind. He just went on hooing and hawing and wheezing and rolling around. After a while his breath gave out, and he sat up and wiped his face and heaved and puffed.

"Tully don't think it was so funny," muttered Lafe.

Tully was still clinging to the tree trunk, like his legs were too weak to carry him back to the others. Mr. Brown had sat down by himself and was talking steadily to anybody that would listen about men getting gored and how you had to shoot a buffalo low down in the lights to kill 'em quick. Mr. Gibbs was still staring after the bull and didn't seem to know any of the rest of them were around. Noah had gone off to look for Tully's rifle, and only his bent back showed in the high grass.

Rice just sat there, grinning and looking dreamy, but after a spell he got up and went over to Tully. Lafe followed. Tully was half standing, half lying

63

against that big old tree. His chest was going in and out like a bellows. "I reckon he was scared plumb out of his wits," Lafe thought. It took a body longer to get over a scare than it did to get over using his legs a mite faster than common.

"You all right?" asked Rice. "He ain't cut you or nothing?"

Tully spat. He glared at Rice, and his eyes seemed to shoot sparks of hate. Without thinking, Lafe stepped back a pace.

"McCay," asked Tully softly, "I reckon you owe me a little something for that show I put on for you. I reckon just any day now you'll have to go find some Injuns to cut you into strips, so's it'll be my turn to laugh. I mean to get me a comfortable place to set, where won't nothing bother me for two, three days, whilst I watch you hurt and suffer. Or maybe they can stretch your torture out for a week just to pleasure me."

Rice's face was solemn as ever now, smooth and brown. "Your shirt's bad tore," was all he said.

Noah came up and handed Tully his rifle. "Here's your gun," he said. "Oh, Tully, I couldn't hardly bring myself to watch. I knowed you was as good as dead. I done had a ringing in my ears, like somebody's death bell, all day long. I just give up on you."

"I seen that," snarled Tully. "Ain't a one of you lifted a hand for me."

Lafe spoke up then. "I couldn't, I didn't have no rifle," he pointed out. "And Rice come out to get the bull just afore he went off and left you. Couldn't nobody shoot whilst you was riding around on him. It was too risky."

Tully stood up straight and snatched his gun out of Noah's hand. For a minute he looked like he might give a swing around with it and knock them all down. His face wrinkled up in disgust. "I ain't fixing to forget this," he said softly. "I hope to see the day when it's just too risky for me to put out a hand to save ary one of you. *Ary* one!"

And he stalked off stiffly.

Five

Lafe swung his ax, and the little sapling fell. He grabbed it before it hit the ground and looked it over. The trunk was straight and sturdy. It would do fine for the scaffold Mr. Gibbs told him to build to put the dressed skins on and keep them safe from rats and other varmints. He stripped the branches from the tree in a few quick strokes and tossed it on the pile with the others he'd chosen.

He straightened up to get the kinks out of his back and wipe off the trash stuck to his sweaty face and neck. Maybe clearing this path to the spring wasn't the thing he ought to be doing right now. There were other matters needed tending to more. But he sure didn't aim to stay in camp. If he had to spend his life clearing a path straight on west to the China Sea to keep away from Tully, he'd do it and never complain.

Tully hadn't spoken one single word since his ride yesterday. He'd sat apart from the rest of them, rubbing grease on his scratches and bruises, stopping every once in a while long enough to glare at Rice and grind his teeth together. Lafe had never seen anybody so eaten up with spite, and it made him uneasy.

The others had gone off hunting early this morning in three separate directions, Mr. Gibbs and Noah on horseback, Rice on foot, and likely they wouldn't be back for several days. Lafe had begun at once to clear this way to the spring. Old Man Brown was poorly and was sleeping the day away on his blanket. So Tully could sit by his lonesome and hate and cuss all he had a mind to.

Lafe bent to his task again. The brush was matted with coils of moonseed. He took his knife and slashed through the vines and chopped away the rest. Beyond was a little patch of cane. He cut it as close to the ground as he could. A sharp cane stob could rip through moccasins and the flesh of a man's foot like a knife and make the worst kind of festering wound. He'd be toting most of the water and wet skins from the spring to the camp, and he wanted the smoothest kind of path.

The ground here was fine and soft as wheat flour, and it grew some of the knottiest, toughest calico bushes he'd ever seen. He swung the ax harder, putting all his strength into each stroke. It didn't bother him to work hard. Ever since he could remember he had done his share of tasks. And he wasn't scared of doing a little more work to make a fine job of something some other body might just have skimmed over quick with a lick and a promise. He always did his best, whatever he set his hand to. Nobody who hired

Lafe Birdwell would ever have cause to complain he didn't do his best.

His mouth went grim. Folks used to say that about his pa. It was his pa who had taught him to take pride in any task, if it wasn't more than carving a wooden paddle to stir soap. Well, what did folks say now? That Samuel Birdwell had made as fine a job of turning traitor and renegade as he had once made of fencing a pasture or weighing a pound of salt or setting figures down in a ledger? Was that what they said?

He wished he knew some way to keep his mind from running on home and his folks all the time, wished the questions about his father didn't pester him all the while. He whacked savagely at one last sweet shrub and stood in the cleared path close to the spring, where it lapped out from under a big flat rock.

Leaning forward on his ax helve, he stared down into the flashing surface and thought how nice it would be to have somebody else look back. Somebody not Lafe Birdwell, whose father had turned traitor and given the rifles and muskets in his store to the Shawnees, weapons and powder and lead that weren't even his, but just trading goods that he was in charge of. That was the same as thieving and bad enough. What was worse yet, it had turned the redskins loose to slash and burn and kill. His pa had as good as murdered half a hundred white men, women, and children.

Lafe clenched his eyes shut hard and drew a deep shuddering breath. It must be true! He didn't want to believe it, but he had to. If it hadn't been the truth, his father would have told him by now. But no word had come in the months since Sam Birdwell had gone off to run the trading store on the Potomac River way to the west of Virginia at the edge of the Indian country. No word had come since the terrible story of the Shawnee raids or since the dreadful day when rumor had first reached the valley that Lafe Birdwell's pa had done this thing. No word had come when the whole neighborhood had turned on the Birdwells, taking vengeance on them for what they figured Samuel had done.

Words had been the worst thing they had used against Mrs. Birdwell and Lafe's sisters. But Lafe and his brother had more than their share of kicks and cuffs and flung rocks. It got where he dreaded going out of the cabin—all of them did. And food ran short, and there was no money. The storekeeper said traitors got no credit from him. Lafe was scared to work in the garden, for folks came out of their way to do him what harm they could. The cow disappeared, and all their neighbors said she must have fallen in a swamp and died, but Lafe wondered.

His ma made up her mind to leave then, and he was glad, though he knew there was no room for him at her sister's place east of the Blue Ridge. He didn't mind striking out on his own. He wanted to do it. He figured he could leave the past behind and not think of it ever again, just as long as his ma and the young 'uns were taken care of.

He'd gone to live with a cousin of his mother's first, away off down the Ridge. And folks had found out all about his pa. He didn't know how. He'd left there and gone on to another cousin's place and then to Uncle George's in Caroliny, and still the story followed. If he could have done it, he'd have changed his name and scarred up his face and shaved off his hair, so nobody would know him. As it was, his name tagged after him wherever he went, so he'd known at last that to escape he'd have to take to the wilderness, where nobody ever came.

When he'd heard about Mr. Gibbs's needing a helper, he'd almost cried for gratitude. For certainsure, here was a way for a boy with no gun and not much knowledge of traps and trails and forest ways to get out in the wilds and away from every wagging tongue. He could even earn a little wage while he was at it.

So here he was a thousand miles from home, way out in the wilderness, sweating and scratched and tired to the bone, and the shadow of what had happened still clung to him, like walnut stains clung to his fingers. Like the stink of a skunk lingered in a body's clothes for months after you'd run into it.

The water was blinding bright where the sun dazzled up from it. Now it was nearly noon, and he was hungry as a barefoot goose. Lafe washed his face and chest in the cold spring and, shouldering his ax, headed for camp. Halfway up the little slope, a grouse came stepping toward him, walking right down the path like it was its very own.

"You watch out now," Lafe told it. "I just might

eat you for supper, you're acting so high and uppity."

"Quit, quit," answered the bird, and slipped into the bushes.

Lafe grinned, swung at a branch he'd missed, then hurried on. Tully was gone. Mr. Brown was up moving around. "You feeling better?" asked Lafe.

"Feeling fine," answered the old man sharply. "Ain't a thing wrong with me. I'm as good a man as I ever was. I just got a little trouble with my eyes. Where's some water? I need me a drink."

Lafe fetched him some water. "There's stew if'n you're hungry," he said. "I mean there's stew less'n Tully ate it all afore he took off. You see him leave?"

"He's been gone an hour or so," the old man told him. "He was in a mean temper, cross as two bears with their tails tied together."

Anyway, he'd left plenty of the stew made from the buffalo Mr. Gibbs had shot late yesterday. Lafe and the old man ate, sitting side by side in the shade of a sugarberry tree. Lafe admired the camp—the way it lay snug against a rocky cliff and then the ground sloped on down to that big spring. Trees enough for shelter and shade, but not so many as to be gloomy or to be in the way. And that big feller

73

over there, the one some storm had halfway uprooted
—the way it leaned, it would make a good place to
scrape skins. He'd flatten and smooth the trunk with
his ax this very afternoon.

It would be fine to stay right here forever, never
to have to go back to a town or a farm and the mean
looks and hateful ways of folks there. It made him
furious the way his pa had wronged them all, for if
he hadn't been a traitor to the frontier folks, he had
certainly betrayed his own family. It wasn't right.

He jumped up suddenly. He wished there was a
way, any way at all, to keep his mind from going on
and on about what had already happened and
couldn't be changed.

"I got work to do," he announced. "Mr. Gibbs told
me a hundred and three things to do afore he got
back. You want some more stew or water or anything
at all?"

"You go on and don't fret none about me," Mr.
Brown said fiercely. "I can take care of myself good
as anybody."

Now what riled him up, wondered Lafe. Tully
must of been dinging away at him before he left.
It'd be just like Tully to hire himself out to take care

of the old man and then bawl out the old feller for not looking out for himself.

By the time the wood was chopped and stacked, the axes and knives sharpened, and the scraping log fixed, it had begun to get shadowy. While he and Mr. Brown ate, the jarflies were running down, and the chittydiddles were tuning up. In spite of the dusk, it was hotter than Tophet. The air was hazy and seemed to hang in Lafe's throat and make it hard to breathe. He could hear the two pack horses down near the creek, ripping away at the cane. Across from him, under the sugarberry, Old Man Brown sighed and heaved on his blanket.

It was stark lonely here, just him and the old man and the dark. He wished he had a rifle. He wished Mr. Gibbs had left him his extra rifle and some lead balls and some powder.

He spread his blanket out beside Mr. Brown's. Even listening to the old man's snores would be better company than nothing. And anyhow, there was the gun. It lay under Mr. Brown's hand with its limp rag trailing from the end of the barrel. If worse came to worst, he could grab it and shoot.

He put out a cautious hand and touched the metal

barrel, and Mr. Brown sat up. "Now you leave that gun be," he muttered. "I don't like folks messing with my gun. Any varmints come around or anything, you just show 'em to me, and I'll shoot 'em. Don't you fret."

Lafe grinned a little. The old man had grit. You had to hand that to him. Thinking about it made him feel a little better, and after a while he fell asleep.

It was barely light when he woke. A red bird was singing from the very top of a poplar. Which-ew, which-ew, which-ew-eewwww. Whirty, whirty, whirty! Lafe stood up and folded his quilt and then walked down to the spring.

It was cooler this morning, but the air felt as sodden and heavy as ever. "Wonder if we're fixing to have a storm?" Lafe asked a mud puppy at the bottom of the spring. It was late in the year for storms, but there was a stormy feel to the day, clabbery, his ma used to call it.

He took a drink and filled a pot to take back to the camp. The old man was still sleeping. Lafe took a piece of cold roast meat and began to chew on it as he mounted the little cliff at the back of camp. From the top of the hill he could see a good piece out over the plain. The long, thin shadows of sunrise deepened and shortened across the meadow.

Some buffalo, maybe thirty or forty, were grazing not a quarter of a mile away. As the light grew stronger, Lafe could make out a few more scattered here and there. Some were cows with calves. The group nearest him were grazing peacefully, their heads all turned in his direction, and a big bull at the front.

Lafe gasped. It looked to him as if that bull had whitish spots on his body. He'd never heard tell of a pied bull. Maybe it was just mud. From this far away he couldn't tell for sure.

Suddenly the bull swung up its head and seemed to stare around and test the air. Its whole big body appeared to stiffen and tense. Then Lafe heard it give a snorting bellow, and the bunch of them began to run. They ran straight, and they ran fast.

It took Lafe a minute to realize they were headed for the camp. There wasn't a thing to turn them aside, to keep them from thundering over the spring creek and smack into camp! And the old man down there, sleeping right in their path!

He ran, yelling as he went, tumbling down the

hillside and across the ledges, bawling his head off. "Git up, git up! They're a-coming. Git up, git up!"

He could hear the roll of their hoofs and the splash as they hit the water. By the time he had scrambled halfway down the cliff, they were roaring through the camp like a river in flood, scattering the firewood, kicking over the stew and the pot of water.

He groaned. The old man—he'd be mashed to a paste by this time. He'd be trampled into a bloody nothing.

As he reached the bottom, there was a sharp crack, and something moved behind the sugarberry tree.

Mr. Brown! The old hunter and his rifle! Lafe yelled out, wild with relief to see the old feller had managed to get out of the way.

But he yelled too soon. The old man turned in his direction and stepped clear of the tree. The last of the buffalo wheeled and lowered its head and came charging toward him, bellowing. It was the pied bull, and its great spotted body filled the whole camping place.

Lafe didn't know how he managed to reach Mr. Brown before the animal did, but he was there first, snatching at the old hunter and dragging him back in among the big rocks that lay at the foot of the cliff.

"It can't get at us, not in here," he thought, but he was wrong. The creature was right behind them, right on their heels, its shaggy head and sharp horns pressing closer and closer.

Six

"Git on! Git on!" panted Lafe. He turned his head to look back at the bull. Rocks rolled under his feet, and he and the old man both nearly lurched to the ground.

"How can I get on with you holding on to me?" demanded Mr. Brown. "You lemme go."

"Hurry!" cried Lafe, pushing and shoving for all

he was worth. There—where that big boulder squeezed up against the cliff—they'd be safe there in that corner. He stumbled toward it, half pushing and half carrying the old man in front of him.

"Watch out!" yelled Mr. Brown, but it was too late. He'd got his rifle catawampus, and it hung up on the rocks, caught him "wump!" across the chest and belly, and well nigh knocked the wind out of him.

Lafe clawed at the gun. "Git it out of the way," he yelled. "He's a-coming!" He could hear the beast's hard hoofs clattering over the rocks right on his heels.

"Leave my gun be!" gasped the old man. "Don't you— Give it here, you fool young 'un!" He snatched it loose.

Lafe squeezed him and the gun in the crack between the cliff and boulder. The old man was skinny and slight. He could slide way back in that little space if he didn't have that rifle. "Throw it away," ordered Lafe. "It ain't no good, anyway. You ain't got powder and lead. Drop it and get on quick." The buffalo was crowding right in with them.

"I ain't fixing to, not on your life," Mr. Brown replied jerkily. "Don't crowd me so," he grunted, as

82

Lafe crushed against him. "I ain't got no room to breathe."

"You'd ought to of left that rifle-gun!" Lafe burst out angrily. "I'm the one on the outside. I'm the one going to get slashed wide open."

He turned his head, and those sharp horns weren't a yard away. The whole place was filled with spotted buffalo, a huge shaggy thing a body might see in the nighttime and think it only a made-up dream-creature. It was real enough now, the bunched-up shoulders, the curved horns, jagged and broken at the tips, the broad wet nose with a patch of pinkish white spread over half of it, the chin whiskers reaching almost to the ground. Matted hair hung down from its forehead, and the yellowish eyes glared out through it.

"Rice says they don't see so good, not something standing still," the boy thought, "but I reckon this here 'un sees me all right. And he don't care for me one bit."

They were safe enough, though. The narrow walls kept it from coming any closer. For a moment more Lafe and the bull stared at each other. Then the animal stepped back a little, twitching its head side-

wise to pull it out of the crack. But it didn't go off. Instead it retreated a couple of steps more and then whammed hard against the opening with its huge forehead. A piece of the cliff shattered and broke off. One of those horns made a deep scar in the boulder. Lafe hollered out and leaned hard on Mr. Brown.

"You're squashing me," the old man wheezed. "There ain't no need to break a body's bones. He can't get in here."

"He don't seem to know that," muttered Lafe.

The bull backed off again, shaking its head. It pawed the ground and then came crashing against the rocks once more. A shower of rubble tumbled to the ground from the cliffside. Lafe cringed. The critter was aiming to butt its way right in and get them. And there was nothing they could do about it but stand and wait for it to happen.

This time when the bull backed away, it turned toward the cliff, and Lafe saw a wound in its neck, where some of the hair had been shed. There was a tiny trickle of blood across the bare place. For the first time he noticed the reddish tinge to the foam dripping from the beast's mouth.

"Why, you done hit him!" he cried. Now wasn't

that something? The old man had shot a buffalo all by his own self. He turned toward Mr. Brown. "Did you hear me? You done hit this here buffalo!"

The old man didn't answer. He had a hand to his head, and he was trembling. "What's the matter?" asked Lafe. The old feller was as white as the inside of a milkweed pod.

Mr. Brown lifted his head. "Nothing," he said quickly. "I'm fine. It's just I can't breathe good all squoze up in here."

"He did breathe kind of quick and ragged," Lafe thought. Yet the boy couldn't give him more room or else he'd be out there with the buffalo. They'd just have to wait for it to go away of its own sweet notion. Unless it would die. He turned back to the bull. No, the old man's bullet hadn't really hurt it, just aggravated it to a fare-thee-well.

He almost panicked. He didn't want the old man to die. And he surely didn't want him to die all jammed up in a crack of the rocks this way, with only Lafe to look after him. It scared Lafe more than the buffalo scared him, thinking about it.

He'd have to get him out of here. The old feller

would be all right maybe if he could lie down for a spell and get his breath good. But how were they going to get out? If this was tomorrow, Rice or one of the others might come back and save them. But it was hardly likely any of them would return so soon, after only one day of hunting.

He kicked the boulder suddenly. Now wasn't this the addle-headed kind of thing that kept happening to him all the time? He reckoned he was the only boy in creation who'd get stuck out in the middle of the wilderness with an old man who didn't have better sense than to shoot at a herd of mad buffalo after the creatures had passed him by and left him unharmed. Nor better sense than to hit one just enough to aggravate the daylights out of it. And Elaphelet Birdwell would be the one who was caught by somebody else's foolishness and had to suffer for it. He kicked again, hard, and hurt his foot and hollered out.

"What happened?" Mr. Brown squeaked out. "What ails you?"

Lafe gritted his teeth so he wouldn't bellow out, "You ail me, you doty-headed old varmint." He

87

swallowed hard. It wasn't any use to get mad or scared or anything. But he had to do something and do it soon.

He squeezed around and looked at Mr. Brown. The old cuss was still mighty white and peaked-looking, but he had strength left to clutch that useless rifle tight against him, like it was all that was going to save him. "And it just might at that," Lafe thought suddenly.

"Mr. Brown," said Lafe. "I'm fixing to climb out of here and fetch back your powder and lead. Then me and you can kill this critter."

The old man perked up a bit at that idea. "Now that'd be fine. It'd be dandy." He touched the wall over his head. "Has it got enough handy-holds?"

Lafe pondered. The boulder went up smooth and straight most places, but the cliff was rough and broken, and there were plants growing out of it here and there.

"I can go up the cliff," he said.

Mr. Brown nodded and scratched around in his skimpy whiskers. "Now go slow," he instructed. "A buffalo, he don't hardly notice nothing long as it don't move fast. A body can just creep along, tippy, tippy, right in front of him and he won't pay no mind."

"I'll go slow as pine sap on a cold morning," promised Lafe. He didn't in reason see that he needed this advice. He was going up the cliff, and the bull couldn't follow.

"Tell you what," Mr. Brown went on. "I'll stick my gun out and wave it around and holler every now and then. That'll draw his attention this way, and he won't pay no heed to you."

"Fine, fine," answered Lafe. Let the old feller think he was helping. It was better than thinking about dying. He felt around for a grip on the rocks over his head. "I'm going. You stay put till I get back."

Climbing was easy at first. When he had trouble, he stopped and braced himself across the crevice, with his feet against the cliff and his back to the boulder. That way he could rest and hunt for handholds. But then the rock walls curved in close together, with only the least little space between them. He had to edge sideways out of the crack and climb along over the open place where the buffalo stood. It didn't matter, though, for he was too high for those horns to reach him.

He began to sidle across the cliff's face on a little ledge just wide enough for his toes, handing himself along, hold by hold, slow and easy. The shelf ended, and beyond that only some roots stuck out for him to clutch. He reached out and grabbed them and tested them cautiously, pulling harder and harder. They held. He slid his left foot ahead of him, moving it up and down, feeling for the best of the holes that pockmarked the wall there. Little bits of rock broke off and flicked onto the ground below.

The buffalo put its head back and bellowed, and the sound echoed against the cliff. Lafe started and jumped. His feet slipped from the crumbling rock, and he was swinging in space, digging frantically at the wall with his toes. He gripped the root with all his strength, but it was no use. His hands slid slowly off the strands. With a yell, he bumped and slithered down the cliff face and landed among the loose rocks at the foot, with his left arm crumpled under him and the breath smacked from his lungs.

The bull stamped forward. Gasping and sobbing, Lafe struggled in among the tumbled rocks, as far back as he could go. His wrist was killing him; pain shot up his arm and made him dizzy as a coot. He turned his face to the ground. He didn't want to see the beast charging at him. He didn't want to see its great hoofs and the gleam of light on its horns.

Mr. Brown's quavering voice shouted out. "Lafe, you there? What happened? Boy, you hurt?"

Lafe waited to get killed and, when it didn't happen, raised his head. The buffalo wasn't even turned toward him. It was watching that white rag on the gun flicking in and out of the crack like some kind of queer bird. Mr. Brown kept hollering and waving for all he was worth. The bull snorted and ran at the rag, butting at the rocks. The rag vanished just in the nick of time. Now the beast stood there, legs planted, head down. Its body shivered with hurt and rage.

So what were the two of them to do now, Lafe asked himself. He wiggled his arm cautiously. It wasn't broken, for a wonder, but it was twisted good, he could tell. It was already beginning to puff up and look bruised.

"What a snibbling mess, for a fact," Lafe told himself. You wouldn't believe you could get into so much trouble in such a short time. Here he was with a sprung wrist and no hope of climbing the cliff, and there was the bull blocking his escape, and there was the old man trapped and thinking Lafe was dead, most likely.

"Lafe! You there?" called out the old hunter piteously.

Lafe didn't know what to do. Let him answer and the bull would turn on him quick enough. If he didn't answer, Mr. Brown might take a notion to step out of that crack and see about him.

The flag poked bravely from between the rocks and flapped about. The bull gave a loud snort and drew back a step or two, and closer to Lafe. It spread its hind legs a little, digging in ready to charge. Lafe could see the big tendons in its hairy hocks. For a second, he could only stare. Tendons! His knife! He could cut those strings with one swish of his knife, and the buffalo would be helpless! His heart pounded. He'd seen many a critter hamstrung. But could he do it? He'd have to.

He got to his knees and jerked out his knife. It was sharp as a briar. He was glad now he'd had all those long lonely times to whet it. He moved his feet up under him in a squat. He would have to be fast, and the knife stroke would have to hard and sure, for there wouldn't be a second chance. That bull could turn like a whirlwind. He picked out a spot right above the hoofs and kept his eyes there. He just stared hard and didn't think about missing.

"Now," he told himself, and sprang forward and slashed in one grand sweep across the hocks. With a roar, the bull spun about, and one black jagged horn swung toward Lafe. He yelled and cowered back. And then the beast leaned and dragged and toppled. Blaring and snorting, it pawed at the ground, trying to rise.

"I done it!" Lafe said aloud in surprise. "I done it proper." His heart was racing so he could hardly breathe. He must be as whey-faced and trembly as the old man.

"Stay there, Mr. Brown," he shrieked suddenly. "Don't come out. I'm all right. I'll fetch the lead."

He flew then on shaking legs. He got the horn and

the leather pouch and was back in no time. The bull was really tearing up the earth, rolling its eyes and screaming in rage and fear. Lafe was almost scared to skirt by it. Mr. Brown looked pale green when the boy led him out into the open. Lafe snatched the rifle and filled the pan.

"Gimme back my rifle-gun," the old man kept gasping.

Lafe had trouble ramming the charge home. His left hand hurt something terrible, and he could hardly hold the weapon, but at last he managed. He handed it back and turned the old man around.

"Now right there is the buffalo," he said. "He's hamstrung, can't get up. You shoot him if you can see him."

"I can see him good," the old man answered indignantly. He tottered a step or two closer.

"You going to be on top of him if you don't stop," Lafe grunted and reached out to grab his arm.

But Mr. Brown was already raising the gun, and his shaking had stopped. He held the rifle steady, and he seemed suddenly bigger and taller—"a mighty hunter, as he must have been in his younger days,"

Lafe thought. He squinted his eyes and took a breath and fired.

The bull shuddered and then sighed. Blood gushed from its mouth and nostrils. "It's dead," the old man said. "Them lung shots get 'em quicker than anything. Can't shoot 'em in the head—too hard."

Lafe knew that. He glanced at the broken rocks and scars at the edge of the crack where they'd been. The tough-headed critter could have battered down the whole cliff, given enough time.

"Rip open the belly for me, boy," Mr. Brown said. "I ain't got the strength."

"Whatever for?" asked Lafe.

"I been dreaming about raw buffalo liver long enough," he replied. "I aim to have it now."

Lafe cut the stomach open, and the old man got down on his knees and reached up inside with the boy's knife and cut out the liver. He sat down with the black mass in his hands and began to eat. Blood ran down his chin whiskers and the front of his shirt, but he ate right on.

Lafe watched. He didn't exactly think he'd like to

join in the feast, but the old feller sure looked to be enjoying it. He didn't look white and shaky any more. He looked fine.

"You done shot your buffalo now," Lafe said suddenly. "You can rest easy."

Mr. Brown stopped eating and looked surprised. "A hamstrung critter?" he asked. "That ain't hunting. That's just slaughtering. I mean to kill me a real bull, on the gallop, if'n I can."

And Lafe couldn't help laughing.

When he had the old hunter safely back at camp, he brought up some of the meat from the buffalo, flitches off the ribs. He hung it from a limb of the sugarberry tree and told the old man he was going to the spring to soak his wrist. "It's swelling bad," he said.

"Boy, I'm right sorry to hear that," Mr. Brown replied. "But it takes more'n spring water to help. Tell you what you do. Get some horse balm. Take the leaves and poultice that wrist." He paused and went on, "Now, I remember one time . . ."

Lafe tiptoed away. The old man could keep him there the rest of the afternoon storifying. But he knew a few tricks; you had to hand it to him. Lafe reckoned that you couldn't hunt in the wilderness all your life and not know some good remedies.

He found the horse balm without too much trouble, a tall, square-stemmed plant with yellowish flowers and a minty smell. He tied the damp leaves around his wrist with a piece of tow. He didn't see how he could do any work now. It was too late to start anything today, anyway. He had settled down at the fire and was roasting a piece of meat when he heard somebody coming.

"It's Mr. Gibbs, I reckon, and he'll make me scrape skins one-handed," he thought grimly.

He turned and saw Tully leading his horse through the trees toward the camp. He hadn't had much luck, Lafe reckoned. He only had a couple of deerskins. Or else he was too mad to shoot. He looked black-browed and sour-mouthed as ever.

"Get them hides to soak," Tully said shortly, dropping the lead line by the boy. "And hobble my horse."

Lafe stuffed his meat in his mouth and swallowed hastily. Tully was in a mood to lambast him a good one if he didn't answer quick. "I'll soak the hides, but I can't hobble no horse," he said, holding up his wrist. He thought he probably could, but waiting on Tully was no part of his job.

Tully seized his hurt arm and twisted till Lafe cried out, and then the man flung his hand away from him. "Did it a purpose to get out of work, I reckon," he sneered. "Injun trick."

Lafe got ready to run. "I ain't hired to you no way," he muttered. "I ain't here to tend to your horse."

"What'd you say, boy?" Tully began, and his eyes blazed up.

Lafe figured he was in for it, but just then the old man squalled out, "Tully, we done killed a buffalo, me and the boy. A big old pied bull."

Tully turned his wrath on the old man. "Who cares?" he growled. "Buffalo ain't no count now. It ain't fit game for a white man to waste his time on. Meat's stringy."

Lafe took to his heels while Tully was looking the other way. He grabbed the skins off the horse and flung them in the spring. The pool wasn't really big enough to take care of a lot of skins, and there'd be a heap of them in time. They had to be kept wet till he could get around to scraping them, else they'd rot. He could dam the stream where those beech roots stuck out into the water. It would be cool, easy work. He'd do it tomorrow. Today was getting on, and he still felt a little dauncy from the fall.

Next morning he waited for Tully to leave, but the man hung around and hung around, snapping and snarling. After a while Lafe took himself down to the spring to build his dam. By midday he'd about finished. He stood up, looking around for another rock. He could hear Tully and the old man talking. Their voices seemed to come and go. They were moving around in the woods, and Lafe wondered what Tully was up to. No good, he'd lay.

He went up the path to the camp. The two of them were gone, but not far. They were crouched behind a bush down at the big creek. The old man had his gun. Had Tully had a change of heart? He must be going to help the old man do some shooting—must have seen a deer coming across the meadow or along the creek. Now Tully had put the old hunter where he could see it coming and shoot it.

Lafe squinted his eyes, searching for the deer. Something moved among the brush across the creek.

Tully pushed at Mr. Brown's shoulders, turning him to get his rifle around in that direction.

Suddenly Lafe saw that was no deer. That was Rice McCay, headed toward the creek with Mr. Brown's rifle pointed smack at him!

Seven

Lafe opened his mouth to yell, but so many frantic words came bubbling up in his brain that he couldn't say any of them. He let loose and ran then, streaking over the ground toward the old man, trying to sound out a warning as he went.

Somebody grabbed him as he lashed through the bushes, somebody wiry and strong. Somebody who held him tight enough around the neck to well nigh cut off his breath, holding his head down and smothering his mouth with a big dirty hand. Tully Brown! Tully was going to let the old man kill Rice, and he was going to keep Lafe from warning him.

"No, he ain't," Lafe told himself.

He *had* to save Rice. He stomped down hard on Tully's foot and jabbed at him with his elbow. Tully tightened his grasp, squeezing the boy's head till Lafe knew it was mashed flat. In red fury Lafe kicked and squirmed and jerked. Tully fought back and tried to twist the boy to the ground. Lafe closed his teeth on as much of Tully's bony hand as he could bite.

Tully swore and dropped Lafe, pushing the boy to the ground with all his strength. Lafe couldn't do anything but lie there and gasp for breath. He saw Tully swing his foot back to bring it crashing into his ribs, and he held up an arm to ward off the blow, but it was his sore one and useless. Tully's toes whammed into Lafe's side like the crack of doom. The man shifted to give him another thump. Lafe rolled, and the second kick almost missed him, landing on his shoulder. It was the one he'd bruised when he fell from the cliff, and Lafe winced and gritted his teeth.

"Tully, what you up to? You done scared off that deer! How come you making all that noise?" the old man squalled out.

Lafe scrambled up then and yelled back at Mr. Brown. "It wasn't no deer! There isn't a deer anywheres around. It was Rice McCay. Tully was aiming for you to shoot Rice."

Tully didn't say a word. He was looking up and around, and his eyes were sort of scared. "Rice'll get him now," thought Lafe. "He'll come busting out of the bushes and beat Tully till he won't have two bones joined together."

"Rice?" the old man said huffily. "I wasn't shooting Rice. I ain't never shot a man. I was shooting at a deer. Tully done spied it for me, ain't you, Tully? It was a deer!"

Tully just went on listening and looking. Lafe watched him wipe a little blood from his hand. "I reckon I got pretty good teeth and jaws," Lafe told himself. "That Tully's got a palm like the underside of a snapping turtle."

The old man fumed, and Tully and Lafe waited.

Lafe knew in reason they were waiting for the same thing, waiting for Rice to come give Tully a grand what-for with the chill off. Lafe rubbed the places where Tully had kicked him. Oh, he was going to enjoy every blow Tully got!

Nothing happened. Lafe's breath came slower, and the blood pounded less in his ears, but he couldn't hear any footsteps or any voice except Mr. Brown's. Tully relaxed. The scared look left his eyes, and he began to grin a little, a mean grin. Lafe edged away from him.

"Rice?" Tully asked. "Where's Rice? Rice wasn't here, wasn't nobody but a little old deer. It must have got fainty-hearted and skittered off when it heard you come busting down that-a-way. What got into you, boy? Ain't you never heared about shooting deer? Even if you're a town boy, you'd ought to know deer-skins don't grow in stores. Surely your pa told you that much afore he passed on."

"It was too Rice," sputtered Lafe, looking wildly around. "I seen him plain."

Or had he? Maybe just the sunlight and shadow and the fact that he was always hoping to see Rice come ambling in had made him see that picture. If Rice was around, why didn't he show himself?

The old man fussed and scolded. Tully looked more and more pleased with himself, like a snake in a nest full of duck eggs.

"Boy, you ought to be ashamed of yourself," Mr. Brown said solemnly. "Old man like me, ain't got long to live, got him a chance to shoot a deer, and you come along and mess things up. I reckon your pa's turning over in his grave this minute to think his son done such a shabby thing."

Tully grinned his sly grin. "I doubt he is," he said softly.

"Mr. Brown, don't you fault me," yelled Lafe. "I done kept you from killing a man. I—" He broke off. It wasn't any use. "Rice!" he turned and bellowed out. "Rice! You there?"

His voice bounded through the woods like a rabbit, jumping from tree to tree, but nothing answered. A big white-billed woodcock rose up from a dead tree and then settled down again.

Tully laughed and spat. "Come on, Old Man," he ordered. "No shooting today. Tom-fool young 'un ought to be bored for the simples."

He led the old man up the path like he was a basket of eggs, like Tully Brown never did a thing but take care of this old cousin and lead him around as carefully as if he was made out of salt and might melt if he got wet.

Lafe watched them go, and then he turned back to the woods. Beyond the shiny stalks of new cane he'd seen Rice, on the path where the light came through the trees in patches of yellow brightness. "Rice," he called again, but only the water answered, a murmur that bubbled off into the stillness.

Well, maybe there had been a deer. It might be he hadn't seen Rice. It might be Tully was just trying to please Mr. Brown.

But no. If Tully hadn't thought Rice was out there, hadn't planned for the old man to murder him, how come he'd looked so scared? And later, how come he'd looked so all-fired pleased with himself when Rice hadn't showed up, hair nor hide?

But if Rice *had* been there, how come he hadn't come out to lay into Tully? He must have seen and heard the whole thing.

Was Rice a coward? Was he a-feared to fight Tully? Lafe had thought Rice was the strongest and best and bravest man in the world. It was hard to think he'd let Tully get away with trying to kill him like that.

Anyway, Lafe didn't aim to go back to camp. Not for a spell. He'd go fetch up the horses. They shouldn't stray so far. No telling when Mr. Gibbs might come back and want his other pack animal.

It didn't take long to find the horses. They liked the cane and followed it along the stream. He found them all—all but Rice's. He searched and searched, till early candlelight almost, and never came on a sign.

He turned back toward camp, and then on the bank of the creek, where the stream from the spring joined it, he saw hoof prints leading away toward the open country. And right beside the hoofs, a man's print, fresh, a man wearing moccasins. Rice! He had been there then. He'd been right there all the time, hearing and seeing everything, and he hadn't come up. He'd cowered in the bushes and let Tully get away with that trick, and then he'd run off, turned tail and gone shivering off, beaten and scared.

In Lafe's chest something seemed to swell up and break. He'd thought Rice was his friend. He'd

thought the hunter was a brave man. Well, he'd been a fool. There wasn't anybody on earth to be Lafe Birdwell's friend, nor anybody he'd ever trust again.

It was good and dark when Mr. Gibbs hallooed the camp and came walking in. He was leading his two pack animals, and they were loaded with raw skins.

"I seen the fire from way out there on the meadow," he said. "I reckon it shines off the cliff there and makes it look so big. I was glad to spy it, for I'd made sure I was lost. But it ain't hardly safe, I don't reckon. There's Injuns about, a whole tribe of 'em, looks like. I seen the frames they used to dry skins and the dead critters they left lying about. You seen any sign of 'em?"

Tully answered. "Naw," he said. "I been out and about, all around, and I ain't come on so much as a toe print. Ain't enough game over this way for the devils, I reckon."

Tully looked so all-fired pleased with himself, it turned Lafe's stomach. He didn't know which was worse, Tully all thunder-faced and sour or Tully grinning like a greased 'possum, thinking he'd got the best of Rice for laughing at him.

"Anyways, he ain't going around bragging about it," Lafe thought. "I reckon even Tully wouldn't brag about how he tried to fool an old blind man into murdering somebody. He'll think of a way to do it though, sooner or later, and he'll make out like he done something smart."

"You done found game a-plenty," Tully went on, pointing at the skins.

Mr. Gibbs's face lit up. "Good Lord a-mighty," he cried. "I come on a salt lick, and I ain't never seen nothing like it. Buffalo—they was jammed in there like kernels on a cob. And they wasn't scared of me a smidgin. I couldn't hardly get the horses through them." He frowned. "And twice I shot deer, and the beasts trampled the carcasses into the mud till there wasn't nothing left of them. Two good hides," he added sorrowfully. "I was plumb scared to try to get 'em. I'd of got trampled sure."

"Great day in the morning!" said Mr. Brown softly. "Don't that sound like heaven? Ain't that enough to make a body's mouth water, just hearing about it?" Lafe saw the old man tremble from head to foot, like a dog that smells bear.

Mr. Gibbs looked happier. "It's a fine place, all

right," he said. "I reckon in two weeks I'll have enough hides to pack up and go home. Two weeks. And every hour bringing more money."

"Money," thought Lafe, leading the horses down to the spring to unload the hides. "If ever I heared tell of a useless thing, it's money." A frog splashed into the water, and then another. A hot, curdled summer moon was rising clear of the trees.

But it wasn't so useless. If he had a little money, he'd buy a gun and some powder and lead and take himself off into the wilderness and never have anything to do with anybody again, never, never!

That moon seemed to give off as much heat as the sun. Later, stewing and sweating, Lafe turned and turned, trying to get to sleep. Then when he did fall asleep, he had all manner of wild dreams. Waking the next morning, he found the water running off him still, the air stifling and heavy, and the sun blurred in a pale sky. It was weather to suit this strange land and the strange way he felt, friendless and alone and empty as last year's mud dobber's nest.

Just the same, there was work to be done. They all worked, even Tully, though he'd lost his easy mood of yesterday. Lafe was glad for plenty to do. It was no hotter stirring than sitting, and if he worked hard enough, he didn't have so much time to think.

His wrist was better, but Mr. Gibbs said he'd build the platform and got Tully to help him. Lafe was glad. He didn't mind doing it, but he figured with his arm bothering him, he might not do too good a job. He didn't want the blame on his head if the thing fell under the weight of all those skins Mr. Gibbs was aiming to put up on it. Let it be on Tully's.

Mr. Gibbs had shot an elk, whose skin was tough and good for nothing but shoes. Lafe had wondered why he'd waste lead on it, but now he saw. They cut it in strips and tied the poles together to make the frame. Mr. Gibbs would never waste a deer hide on such. Lafe wished he'd brought home some of the meat. He'd heard elk steaks were fine. And they were almost out of meat fit for food, it spoiled so quick in this heat. But Mr. Gibbs never thought about packing back any meat, not when he could carry skins worth money.

Lafe did his chores and then set to the task of scraping the skins. He fetched a soaked hide out of the pool and spread it over the sloping tree. He took one of Mr. Gibbs's big butcher knives and thrust the point deep into a block of wood, so it had two handles.

Scraping wasn't so hard, it just meant running the knife blade over the wet hide to shave off the hair. But you had to watch not to scrape too hard and make a hole. It made Lafe impatient, a little, to have to go so slow and careful, but he wanted to do a good job.

When the hair was off, he flipped the skin over and did the fleshing, cutting off the bits of meat and fat that still clung. The least little bit left could rot a hide, and one bad hide could mortify a whole pack. Did that happen, Mr. Gibbs would use Lafe's own pelt for a replacement, Lafe felt sure.

He spread the finished skin on the grass and went to fetch another. He wasn't wearing anything but his linsey britches, and he dipped in the creek to wash off the itchy hair and the fat and to cool a little. He'd never known such weather before. Going naked was hardly any more comfortable, and the skeeters ate him up, but he didn't want that mess all over his one good shirt.

By noon he was standing ankle deep in hair and the slush from the dripping hides, and Noah came riding in with more skins. He was glad to see Noah, who was almost always good-natured. He'd brought meat, too, a fresh-killed deer. Noah liked to eat, and he was a good cook, a lot better than Lafe. He had a little black cooking pot he thought a heap of and always kept by him. Once on their journey he'd forgot it, left it sitting all forlorn by their dead camp fire, and had walked miles back to get it. And he knew about what wild things to put in the pot so deer meat didn't always taste like deer meat. Ramps and sage and such as that.

Mr. Gibbs came up and looked over the skins Lafe had finished and made sure his initial was cut in the leather somewhere. He didn't say anything, and Lafe figured that was a compliment. If there'd been something he didn't like, he'd have said plenty.

"I'm a-leaving," Mr. Gibbs announced finally. "I don't aim to be gone but two days. You get them skins dried and up on that scaffold. Weight 'em down good, now. Don't forget. And cover 'em with that buffalo hide. We're bound to have a little rain soon. Can't keep up this hot without it rains."

Noah stared up uneasily at the yellowish sky. "Peers to me we're fixing to have more than rain," he said. "Looks like a storm for sure."

Mr. Gibbs shook his head. "Too late in the year for storms," he answered and he rode off.

After a while Tully left, too, without a word. Old Man Brown was napping away, and Lafe and Noah had the place to themselves. Noah helped a little with the skins and fetched the water and did the cooking, and Lafe was grateful. Noah was good company. He kept jawing away about his sister and his nephews that he took care of, for their husband and father was dead.

"Shawnees killed him," explained Noah. "Some fool let 'em get hold of some whisky and guns, and they come a-raiding and killed my sister's man. It was wicked, putting guns in Injuns hands."

Lafe felt that old scared shock, right down to his marrow, but he just went on scraping.

Noah went on talking. He tried to tell Lafe a tale about a hollow tree so full of squirrels that it busted open and spewed out a rain of squirrels, but he got so mixed up and twisted that Lafe laughed more at Noah than he did at the story.

Next morning Noah got his things together and readied himself to ride off once more. "I wouldn't go," he said uncertainly, "except Aquilla done said it was too late for a storm. Me, I made certain it was going to storm, and bad, too."

Lafe himself thought something bad was bound to happen. There wasn't a trace of wind down on the ground. It was fever-hot and breathless, but overhead the clouds, sulfurous and wicked-looking, boiled and scudded. The sun showed red and sullen through the clouds, and the heat folded over them like a coverlid.

"But I always listen to Aquilla," Noah went on. "He's got book learning, Lafe. You know that? Ain't often I get to go out hunting with a feller smart as him."

Lafe couldn't see what book learning had to do with it. He didn't reckon Noah knew, either. It was just something that popped into his head, and he blurted it out without thinking.

Noah mounted and rode away, turning to call, "I'll bring you back some buffalo tongues, and we'll cook 'em wrapped in sassafras leaves."

Lafe waved. He was sorry to see Noah go.

The weather seemed to have a bad effect on Mr. Brown. He got up crotchety and snarled at everything, almost like Tully. "Must run in the family to be mean," Lafe thought. "Poor old feller, he hadn't ought to be out here. He ought to be setting home fanning himself with a turkey wing."

The morning wore on. It got so hot that Lafe had to stop working. The least little thing made him pant. The stench from the pied bull floated into camp, so strong you could almost see it, and mixed with the stink of wet hides, it was more than he could stand. He went to the spring and took the old man with him. It was cooler there, and the smell didn't burn into his nose as it had.

The old man was leaning over wetting his face with the water when the wind sprang up. He lifted his head and said, "We'll get rain now."

"I better go cover them skins," Lafe muttered, and leaped up the path. He climbed the platform, dragging the heavy buffalo hide with one hand.

The wind died. It was as still and hot as ever. Lafe looked up. Wasn't it going to rain after all? Surely it was. The sky was such a dark, curious yellow. Over there the clouds gathered in such a whirling mass. He bent to his work.

He spread out the skin and weighted it with a

couple of little logs. It was a queer day, and no mistake. There just didn't seem to be any air, like it was being all sucked up and away from the earth. And the light was such a strange, dirty green color, and everything sounded so funny. Way off there was a whining buzz, like all the bees in the world, coming closer. He raised his head again. What was that queer noise? How come it made his hair prickle out all over his head? How come it was growing louder and coming nearer and nearer?

And the sky! The sky was falling down on top of him!

Eight

The wind hit him like something solid, like a roof beam or a rock had whopped him all of a sudden. He managed to grab the platform and hold on while the gale seized him and whipped him around like he was no more than the rag tied to Mr. Brown's gun. He made sure his arms would be jerked from their sockets.

The roar was terrible. It was all about him one moment, and the next it had battered in one side of his head and went screeching around inside his skull.

He got a glimpse of a greenish-black mass of clouds come spinning over the meadow. As it went, it caught up the dust and brush and dry stalks of cane and drew them up in a long, twisting rope. Lafe knew in reason it would catch him, too. In a minute he was going to go twisting and wheeling up into the sky and never be heard of again. He was a goner. Nobody nor nothing could save him.

Then a rain of leaves, sand, and sticks hurtled at him, stinging his face and bare body. Great branches, like huge green birds, soared past. The wind grew stronger. Trees bent and swayed, and one great beech snapped off in the middle of its trunk, like it was no more than a rotten twig. The top of the sugarberry splintered; branches and chunks of wood exploded in all directions.

He couldn't get his breath. The wooden platform rocked and reeled under him like a bucking horse. Still he held on, clutching those thin strips of saplings for dear life. The logs weighting the skins went arrowing off into space, and the skins followed. One of them wrapped itself around Lafe's head, and he bawled in terror, though his voice stayed down in his lungs.

The wind scraped the hide off, and it went sailing away. Lafe still held onto the platform, though he was so dizzy that he seemed to be flying off behind the hides and logs. He felt like he was flying. Oh, great day in the morning, he *was* flying! The scaffold was no longer rooted in the ground but had been torn loose and was now riding along with everything else the wind had swept up, and Lafe was going with it. Twisted parts of the framework swirled around him. He let go the piece he was holding and right away wished he hadn't. He was banged, whirled, and thumped and rolled over and over in the air. Sometimes the ground was far above him, or it stretched off to one side out of reach.

In terror, he tried to strike out with his arms, the way he would swim a creek, but nothing helped, and he went tumbling and spinning over and over into the middle of some flattened button bushes that scratched and pulled at him till he was caught and lay still. His eyes were open, but he couldn't see a thing. He had to struggle for breath, and he figured

he was dead, killed by the hurricane and left. The wind roared over his head like a big beast anxious to tear open his chest and suck out his insides. He couldn't move hand nor foot. He had so little strength, he couldn't even yell out his fright.

At last he managed to get his lungs full of something, mostly grit and dust it felt like, but it helped. The red haze faded from in front of his eyes, and he could even raise a shaking hand and wipe the sweat from his face. The gale was dying down, and a slashing mixture of rain and hail had begun to fall. Lafe rolled over in the button bushes and retched up his breakfast, while the big drops and sharp pellets of ice struck on his head and bare shoulders.

After a while he sat up and felt better. "Reckon I'm pretty dern tough," he thought, looking at the scratches on his body. "Can't nothing get the best of me, not Tully nor buffalo bulls nor hurricanes nor nothing." He was mighty pleased with himself and looked his fingers and toes over to be sure they were all there. He was worried about his ribs, though; he had a notion the wind had chewed up just a heap of them and gone off with the rest.

He crouched with bowed head till the hail stopped

and the rain eased a little. Then he looked up, feeling lightheaded and queer, like he'd had a fever for a month of Sundays. He didn't have the dearest notion where he was. For all he knew, he might have been blown back to Virginny. And even if there were any landmarks around, he'd never recognized them, not in this mess of broken trees and piles of wet leaves and brush. It all looked strange, not like a real place at all.

And—and what in the nation were these things bearing down on him, these big, pink, long-legged, bloody-headed, queer-shaped things coming straight at him?

The creatures didn't seem to see him. They came right on, as though he weren't there. He couldn't get to his feet, he couldn't get out of their way, he couldn't do anything but wait there, gaping, till the things ran right over him with fierce beaks and raking claws. He yelled and slapped and beat at them, and they fled on, all but one.

This awful-looking beast seemed bound to jump up on top of his head. He flailed out at it and got it by a tuft of grayish fur on its back, and it made a strangled, gargling noise. The fur came off in Lafe's hand, and he saw it was feathers. The animal gave a little jump up in the air, waving stubby arms, and then streaked away.

Awe-struck, Lafe looked after the birds. Turkeys! Turkeys with their feathers stripped off by the wind, turkeys driven plumb crazy with fear and running through the woods all naked like that. Naked turkeys! Who would believe such a thing?

The rain had almost stopped, but sheets of blue lightning played back and forth over the clouds, and every once in a while a stream of fiery balls sprayed down toward the earth. That little hill, the one behind their camp, that was one thing the wind hadn't been able to change. Against the flashing sky it looked mighty comforting and familiar to him. Now he knew where he was after all. He got to his feet. He was worried about the old man. That wind just might have picked up a skinny little feller like him and whirled him away to kingdom come.

He made his way through the down trees toward the spring, calling in between the rolls of thunder, "Mr. Brown. Oh, Mr. Brown, you there?"

Down by the rock where the spring flowed out, a big lump of trash rose suddenly and began to move.

Lafe jumped and took a step backward. Awful things kept happening. Here was water and sticks and grass and leaves shaped like a man, leaping up at him. It was enough to give a body the shakes. Even after he saw it was the old hunter, he kept feeling queer for a moment or so.

"Mr. Brown!" he cried, running toward him finally. "You all right?"

The old man was trembling, but his eyes peeped out bright and lively from between the weeds he was wearing. "I'm most nigh froze," he said shakily. "But I ain't hurt none, and I still got my rifle."

"You got down in the spring!" exclaimed Lafe admiringly. "I reckon that was a mighty good place to get. Did you ever in your life see such a wind? That must of been the worst storm in creation."

"Naw!" The old man was scornful. "I seen storms in my time blew so hard, they blew the wells inside out. This 'un warn't nothing. Son, we got to get us a fire—I got a little chill down in that there water."

Lafe was chilly himself without his shirt, but he didn't figure fire-making was going to be easy, everything wet as it was and their possessions all blown away. He began to hunt around.

Food was easy come by, for birds and small animals of every sort lay about in the woods, dead or dying. At the foot of the cliff behind the camp, the game lay ankle-deep, most of it bashed against the rocks so hard it had burst into smithereens and wasn't worth picking up. Doves and pigeons, turkeys and ducks, all kinds of birds. And rabbits and 'coons and foxes and 'possums, and a wolf with his skull cracked wide open. It was kind of a grisly sight, and Lafe shuddered, for the wind could just as easily have whapped him up against the cliff and left him among the rocks with his liver and lights splattered about.

He lucked upon a wallet, one of Mr. Gibbs, with flint and steel and a piece of dry tow inside. He was sure glad to find it, for it was getting on to nighttime. The fire had just begun to blaze good when Tully came wandering in. He'd lost his horse, and a limb had hit him in the head and blacked both his eyes and gouged a hunk out of his cheek. Lafe wouldn't say he rejoiced in Tully's misfortunes; it was just that if it had to happen to somebody, Tully was the one he'd pick to have it happen to.

Lafe kept the fire built up high all night, and they all slept warm enough. The next day he found his shirt and the old man's powder horn busted open and empty. Tully turned up an ax and Mr. Brown's blanket and a skillet. Lafe reckoned with a heap of looking all their gear and belongings could be found in time, maybe most of the skins, too. But he was worried about the others and went up on the cliffside, hoping to see some sign of them. He figured he'd probably never see Rice again, now that he'd run off. Still he hoped he was safe, for he didn't wish the young hunter any harm. But Noah and Mr. Gibbs ought surely to be heading back here.

The real storm path hadn't touched the camp. It had gone by a good piece away from the lower side of the hill. He could trace its track through the tall grass and the cane and where it went wiggling off through the woods, a wide road with not a tree left standing. He was sure glad he hadn't been in there.

He didn't see any of the men. He loped down the hill and back to camp. He wanted to clean out the spring and build back his dam. Later in the day, Mr. Gibbs came in with his horses. He'd been a long way off when the hurricane hit, hadn't got more than a hard breeze and some heavy rain. He couldn't seem to believe all the damage the camp had suffered. He kept looking around and shaking his head in a baffled sort of way.

"Whom the Lord loveth, He chasteneth," he said finally, but his eyes were angry, Lafe thought, and he made up his mind to stay out of reach of Aquilla Gibbs's hard hand. Mr. Gibbs didn't have to love you a bit to chasten you plenty.

Every day after that, Lafe set out to look for their belongings. A few of the things had collected in bunches against the cliffwall and at the roots of the biggest trees still left standing. He found most of the skins that had been soaking in the pool. They had washed downstream a good ways and then caught on some trees that had fallen into the creek. He chanced upon a few of the half-dressed skins. They were stiff and damp, but a little sunning and lots of rubbing them back and forth against a tree would make them soft again. But he was amazed at how far away the skins had blown.

One of the things he came on was Noah's little black pot, sitting all by itself, with its lid on in the middle of some flattened-down cane. "It looks plumb

cheerful and comfortable there, like a fat little person," Lafe thought, and remembered a riddle his
mother used to ask:

> Hoddy Toddy
> Has a round body,
> Three feet and an iron hat,
> Now what do you make of that?

Lafe picked it up and went on. But he worried a
little about Noah. He should have been back at the
camp by now; it was the end of the third day after
the storm. Was he out looking for his little pot?

There were a heap of things to see, Lafe thought,
enough to keep a body stopping and mirating and
wondering for a long time. Maybe that was what
Noah was doing. Maybe, like Lafe, he'd come on
trees with branches stuck into the trunks like arrows
or some turned clean upside down with their roots
high overhead. Or a buffalo with its eyes pulled
plumb out of their sockets by the wind. A thing like
that now would give Noah something to ponder on
for the rest of his life.

Lafe wished he had time to spend on such wonders
himself. He wished he was out here without the

others. Just himself, with his own gun and powder and shot and nothing to worry about. Not Tully or Mr. Gibbs or what in the world he was going to do with himself when the hunt was over and whether he might have to go back to Uncle George's or somewhere else.

There were dead beasts and varmints all about. Buzzards flocked overhead by the hundreds and rose in a black cloud when Lafe came near them on the ground feasting. Sometimes he could hear them talking together in their harsh hissing voices, and it gave him the creeps.

Mr. Gibbs had near about run himself to death the first day after the storm, trying to salvage all the deerskins he could. It had made Lafe laugh out when he spied Mr. Gibbs, sweating and panting as he stumbled along trying to get to the carcasses before the buzzards and the wolves. But it had been a wise thing to do, Lafe had to admit, for they'd lost so much. Even a half hide that was worthless at the trading store could make a good long rawhide rope or patches or a pair of moccasins to replace the ones they'd lost.

Lafe himself was going barefoot. He didn't mind;

he was fair used to it. His ma used to say wearing moccasins was just a decent way of going barefoot. Anyway, his soles were tough as whang leather. Yet he was careful in the broken cane. He knew from bitter experience how dangerous cane could be. But mostly he could walk on anything and hardly feel it.

He was thinking about that when he saw a pair of moccasins lying by a sycamore tree, a big hollow tree that must have blown over in the storm.

"Well, forevermore," he thought, "it may be they're mine." He put the little pot down and ran forward.

But the moccasins weren't by themselves. They stuck out from the hollow tree at a strange angle, and they were on somebody's feet. Lafe turned cold with dread. He didn't need to touch the man to know he was dead. He eased the body out of the tree onto the moss and rolled it over.

Nine

Noah's eyes were sunk in his head, and his mouth was pinched in. There didn't seem to be a mark on him, but the tree was splintered and twisted. Maybe lightning had struck it and killed poor Noah, or maybe the tree had crunched him somewhere inside as it fell. Or maybe he'd just died of fear.

Lafe's eyes filled with sudden tears. Poor old

simple-minded, good-hearted Noah! And who would take care of his sister's boys now?

He reached out and pulled Noah's shirt together and tied it around him. Then he tried to cross his hands on his breast, but the arms were too stiff. He'd have to try to bury him. He couldn't let the wolves and buzzards at him.

He got up and began looking around for the best place. Down by the creek the dirt would be soft under the moss. Still, with only a knife, it would take a long time and a heap of digging. Maybe he ought to go back to camp and fetch the others back with him to help put Noah in the ground proper. But the others wouldn't trouble themselves. He was sure of that.

"If it gets done, it'll have to be me," he said aloud.

He'd have to make do with what was here. He could put Noah right back inside the tree, and he'd have a fine sycamore coffin, good as pine any day. And instead of digging a hole, he'd just have to cover the log where it was.

He pushed the body back inside and plugged up the end with rocks. Then he heaped up more and more logs and rocks on top. He worked harder than he had to, for a fact. With all the carcasses lying around for the picking, the wolves weren't likely to bother themselves to dig under all these logs. But it was the last thing he could do for Noah to make certain his rest wouldn't be disturbed.

When he was done, he fetched some bright yellow and purple flowers and stuck them in the little pot and set it by the cairn. It looked so pitiful that he almost wished he hadn't done it, and he turned around quickly and headed back for camp.

He stopped after a while, watching a buffalo butt again and again at another one killed in the storm. He wished he had a rifle. He could shoot the critter from here, he was certain. As much as he'd listened to the old man talk, he knew just where to shoot. He wondered what had happened to Noah's gun. He'd never thought to look around the sycamore for it.

A little closer to camp, he came on a knife, stuck in the ground by the handle, with the blade standing up. He might have run against it and lost a toe or two had he not seen the sun glint on it. There was a nick in the blade, but he could whet that out. On further, he found a deerhide with the letters AG in one corner. It was so ripped and torn, it wasn't good for a thing, and he didn't want to bother to fetch it along. He glanced around to make sure nobody was here and then threw it into a clump of tall ironweed and hurried on again.

You could see the camp plain against the cliff, now that so many of the trees on the slope were gone or broken off or stripped of leaves. Lafe wondered if Mr. Gibbs knew how that scaffold and the skins on it stood out. The place used to be hidden among all the greenery, but now it was easy seen from almost any direction. They ought to move into a safer place likely.

When Mr. Gibbs saw Lafe, he began to bawl him out for wandering in the woods, like Mr. Gibbs himself hadn't been the one to send him out there and tell him to hunt up their truck.

Lafe let him holler for a while, and then he spoke up finally. "Noah's dead," he interrupted. "I come on him in the woods, and I buried him."

Mr. Gibbs stared a minute at his hired boy, and then he said, "The Lord giveth and the Lord taketh away. Dust to dust. You bring in his gun?"

Well, that was Mr. Gibbs's way, and he couldn't help it, Lafe reckoned. He shrugged. "I didn't see no gun. I didn't see nothing of his'n, only that little pot he made so much of."

"You should of brought it," Mr. Gibbs scolded. "We could use it."

Lafe didn't see why. Pots were one thing they had. The wind had just rolled them to the foot of the cliff and left them. Anyway, Noah's pot was hardly big enough to get a knuckle bone in. But Mr. Gibbs always liked to hang on to anything, you could depend on it.

"What about his skins?" Lafe asked suddenly. "You want me to dress 'em? You going to take 'em back to his sister and her boys? Reckon they'll need the money, now he's gone."

"His sister?" Mr. Gibbs looked disgusted. "He ain't got no sister. He had a brother had a whole gaggle of children over on Peavine Ridge, but they never did have nothing to do with Noah. He just liked to make up them tales about how he had a lot of folks, on account of he didn't have wife nor child of his own. Naw, his skins are mine now, I reckon, and you dress 'em along with the others."

Lafe didn't know whether to believe all that or not.

It would be like Noah to invent a sister to have something to talk about. But it would be like Mr. Gibbs to say there wasn't a sister, just so he could take the skins. Lafe shrugged. There wasn't anything a hired boy could do about it. Since it was Mr. Gibbs's hunt, he reckoned his master had as good a claim to the skins as anybody.

He set to work again, graining the hairy side of the pelts and fleshing off the underneath. It was the same old work, but it all seemed different now, what with Rice gone and Noah dead. And the camp had changed up so, the big sugarberry broken to bits, and the tree trunk Lafe used for scraping skewed around a different way from what it was and so wobbly as to be almost useless.

There was a difference in the weather, too. The September days were fine, bright, and hot, but not heavy, airless-hot, the way it had been before the storm. Lafe sort of figured he'd never be easy in that kind of weather again, and even yet, let the wind rise a little bit, and he got the shakes.

The nights were cool; Lafe was glad of that. He worked so hard during the day, though, he had a notion he'd have slept through the hottest kind of night. Hard work never hurt a body, and it kept him from thinking too much about his dismal troubles, about his father and his home that had disappeared, about Rice and the coward way he'd run off, and about Noah, dead and buried.

Tully and Mr. Gibbs went in and out, hunting all the time. The piles of skins mounted. Once Tully took Mr. Brown out, and the old man shot a buffalo on the gallop. Or so he claimed, and Tully swore it was the truth. Lafe knew Tully wouldn't mind lying the least little mite, but it was kindly of him to do it for the old feller. Lafe was glad for Mr. Brown and took the extra trouble of dressing the buffalo skin, worthless though it was.

Mr. Brown wanted to take it home as proof of his skill. "I'll have a heap to tell folks back home," he said proudly.

Lafe stopped dead still. With the fleshing knife in his hand, he stood there like he'd been frozen and stared at the piles of hides ready for sale to some store-keeper. Back home! He'd let the thing creep up on him, hadn't wanted to think about it, didn't, for a fact, quite know what to think, for they would be leaving any day now. Mr. Gibbs figured the hides at two pounds each, so that meant no more than a hundred loaded on each horse. There were already over three hundred hides here, with plenty more raw ones soaking in the creek. He'd have to stop dressing them soon, for they only had four horses now. They'd never found Noah's, and Rice had gone with his.

Lafe set to work again. What was he going to do? There was no call to seek out his mother. She was living on others' kindness and could offer him nothing, and the thought of going back to Uncle George's was mortal hateful to him. He wasn't certain Uncle George cared to have him again, anyway. Oh, if only Rice had stayed, then he might have persuaded the young hunter to take him deeper into the wilderness. Maybe to the West, where there were no folks, and the trees and trails wouldn't care what your name was or what your father had done.

But Rice was long gone from here. He'd run off to save his own skin and never cast a backward glance at Lafe Birdwell. Of a sudden, it came over Lafe that he'd depended a lot on having Rice and Noah around at this point of the journey. The hard work over and done with, there wasn't a reason in the world why Mr. Gibbs and Tully shouldn't leave him out here for the Cherokees and the wolves, and not a soul to say them nay. Nobody back in Caroliny knew where he was. There was not a person to ask his master about that bound-out boy he took with him when Mr. Gibbs returned home. Only Mr. Brown might ever again mention him, and folks would figure it was his addled old brain making up some tale.

Now that was foolish. Mr. Gibbs was close, but he wasn't wicked. He wouldn't leave a boy out here to die. Not without a reason.

Well, he'd have a reason—a good one. In his heart Lafe was certain Tully knew the truth, and he aimed to tell Mr. Gibbs. It might be he already had. Lafe had a notion Mr. Gibbs could decide in no time at all that it would be sinful to pay good wages to a traitor's child. And the best way to keep from paying him wages would be to leave him behind.

Such thoughts scared Lafe. They scared him so bad that his knife went in deeper than he'd aimed for it to, and there was a hole in the skin. And Mr. Gibbs took that minute to look over his shoulder. He bellowed like a buffalo bull and fetched Lafe a smack over the ear that made the boy see stars.

Tully laughed, and it was all Lafe could do not to run over and kick him. He gritted his teeth and clutched the knife and thought about how he'd like to squeeze Tully's dirty neck that hard, squeeze till all his teeth came popping out. He didn't blame Mr. Gibbs. He was paying good silver and board for his work, and he had a right to be ireful over losing a hide. But Tully—

After a spell he went on working, taking a deep breath every now and then to try to quiet the pounding of his heart. Tully passed by and sneered, "You can't do nothing right, orphan. I reckon Aquilla's glad he don't have to put up with your worthless ways much longer." Lafe didn't look up. He put all his mind onto holding the knife steady.

That night he thought he heard Tully and Mr. Gibbs talking long after dark, sitting out of the fire's reach and muttering together. They were making their plans now; he knew they were. He could imagine Tully grinning at what the Indians and the wild beasts would do to Lafe Birdwell, how he must be laughing and nudging Mr. Gibbs and telling him it was good riddance, the boy would be bare bones within a week after they left him, with nobody in the settlements to care.

He couldn't let them do that. He'd outsmart them. He'd leave first. Tomorrow night he'd take his knife and quilt, some deer meat, and one of Mr. Gibbs's guns. It wouldn't be stealing. He'd take it and some powder and lead in place of his wages, for he'd earned his wage honestly and worked as hard as he knew how.

He had shot his pa's gun enough to be able to handle one of his own, he felt sure. Though he was a better farmer than woodsman, he'd learned a lot on this journey, and tough as he was, he knew he could get along all alone in the wilderness. It seemed to him he'd been doing all right in taking care of himself for some time now, and he could go on doing it. He'd build him a shelter somewhere against the winter coming on, line it inside with bearskins and buffalo hides. He'd be warm and snug, and life would be sweet as maple honey. There'd be nobody to bother and torment him like Tully, nor whop him like Mr. Gibbs. His troubles would be far away in the settlements, and he'd live happy and content by his lonesome.

All the next day he planned how he'd do it. Mr. Gibbs kept him on the run, fetching the skins down off the scaffold, folding and tying them in bundles. Still his head kept figuring out how he'd lay hands on the extra rifle of Mr. Gibbs, the one he kept wrapped amongst his truck, how much powder and lead he would carry, and which way he'd go when he left here in the darkness.

He did so much toting and fetching and so much thinking that he was worn out by nightfall and slept the night through without once stirring. Tully and Mr. Gibbs were up before he was the following morning.

"Tonight," Lafe promised himself. "I'll do it tonight. I won't go to sleep a-tall. I'll stay awake till they're sleeping good and then leave."

He didn't know how everything happened so quick after that. One minute he'd been scraping a skin, and the next he was loading bundles on the horses. The last hide, still damp, was flung over the others, and their blankets and skillets were hastily

tied on with the packs. He just hadn't reckoned they'd be ready to move out of there so soon. There were a few raw hides still soaking in the pool. Who'd have thought Mr. Gibbs would be willing to leave them? But the horses were already staggering under their loads. Even Mr. Gibbs must have known he'd be a fool to try to make them carry any more over the rough homeward trail.

Mr. Gibbs was full of bustle. Lafe could see he hadn't loaded skins on the horses, he'd loaded silver shillings, all shiny and clinking. And Mr. Brown was as pert as he'd been yet, fretting to get home and tell the folks for miles around all he'd done. Only Tully was sullen and silent as ever, letting little glints of meanness flash out of his eyes every time he looked at Lafe.

"They ain't said nothing about leaving me," Lafe thought. "But I don't aim to give them that pleasure. I got to get and get fast."

He glanced around. Tully, with his back to Lafe, was fixing the pack saddle on his horse. Mr. Gibbs was scouting around the sugarberry for anything they might have forgotten. And there was Mr. Gibbs's rifle he'd left lying on a stump. This was Lafe's chance. It was now or never. He slipped over ready to pick it up and be off into the woods. Just then a big copper-colored hand reached out from behind the stump and grasped the rifle.

Ten

For the space of a breath, Lafe hoped it might be Rice, his hand was almost that rough and brown. Rice might come back to see how Lafe was getting along, he just might. Lafe longed for it to be true, but to know different, he had only to raise his eyes to the blue and gold bangle around the man's arm and to the shirt, grimy and torn but ruffled and lace-trimmed and tied with a fancy ribbon at the neck. His heart banged and bumped, and his belly tightened into knots. Injuns!

He had had it in mind to say something to Mr. Gibbs the other day about how the storm had showed the camp and scaffold plain, so anybody could see that—right out here in Cherokee country—a band of foolish white men had dared to come hunting where they had no right to be. Now they had been spied out. Here were the red men, thick as flies at a burial. Nobody said a thing; none of the white men moved. They just seemed to know all of a sudden that the camp was circled by the savages.

The Cherokees strolled in as if the place was theirs, and Lafe reckoned it was. Fine young men, with all kinds of ornaments looped from their ears and twisted in their scalp locks, in fancy clothes or wearing breechclouts and leggings; older men, pot-bellied and round-faced, but still plenty mean-looking and fierce, in bright calico and dirty deerskins and every kind of dress. There were some women along, and seeing them, Lafe reckoned what he'd always heard about them was true. They were the worst when it came to torturing prisoners. These were as strong-looking and cruel-faced as the men; their eyes looked cold and spiteful. Lafe shivered when their glances touched him. He was scared.

The women began to lead the horses off right away, and Lafe figured the Cherokees must have waited till everything was packed and ready to go before they stepped in. Now all they had to do was collect the rifles and powder horns, and the whites wouldn't have a thing left.

Lafe slid his eyes around at his master. Mr. Gibbs looked like somebody who'd just been hit hard on the head. He stood there dazed and disbelieving. Once or twice he opened his mouth and kind of gulped, but he didn't say anything. Tully cowered against a tree; his face was dirty green. He held his rifle in his hand, but when one of the warriors took it from him, it slipped out of his grasp like he was a dead man already and couldn't work his muscles to hold onto it.

Only Mr. Brown looked to give the red men any trouble. When one of the savages seized his gun, he held on like a snapping turtle and was jerked this way and that. The brave grabbed the gun then by both ends and held it high, and the skinny little old

149

hunter dangled from it like nothing more than the white rag tied to the barrel.

"Leggo!" he gasped. "I done had this rifle fifty years. Ain't nobody but me ever laid a hand to it. Leggo!"

The brave gave the gun a shake or two, and the old man's hands slipped a little. When the Cherokee slung the weapon, whirling around on his heels, Mr. Brown went sailing away and crumpled on the ground. But he went right on hollering, "Greasy varmints! Give it back, give it back!" The Indian snatched off the rag and threw it after the old hunter.

The women laughed a heap at all this, standing around holding their sides and shaking, and the men grinned. They seemed in a peaceful mood, and Lafe hoped to goodness they stayed that way. Only one old man on horseback looked as solemn as a judge where he sat his horse at the edge of the camp. The horse was decked out to a fare-thee-well, with a fancy bridle and saddle, what had once been a white man's saddle, and a fine one at that. The stirrups were gone, and the old Indian's feet in their worn moccasins dangled at his horse's ribs.

He just sat and watched all the while, only stirring to wave on those leading off the pack horses. A few of the warriors followed the animals. Were they really all going to leave? Lafe had never heard of Indians kind enough to let white prisoners go unharmed. All the stories told in Virginny said redskins beat and mangled and burned their captives, and if there was anything left after that, they sliced them in thin pieces to feed to their dogs.

Lafe still had his knife. He turned away a little so it wouldn't be seen. If they really left, his knife might save them all from starving. There wasn't anything he couldn't do with it. But right away a brave sauntered over to the boy and held out his hand. He had a huge nose, black and hooked as a buzzard's beak. Lafe gave him his knife quick. He didn't care to tangle with this one.

The old chief clapped his hands once, and all the Cherokees began to leave. Mr. Gibbs made a noise like those bare turkeys Lafe had run into during the storm. He sprang toward the rider and seized him by one dangling foot. "Don't take 'em all," he begged. "Leave me half. That's fair, ain't it? I done shot and skinned 'em. Let me have just half."

The Cherokee looked down at him scornfully. "My land. My deer. My skins. Not your land. Not your nothing."

He pulled his ankle out of Mr. Gibbs's grasp and placed his foot on the white man's stomach and pushed. Mr. Gibbs went staggering back and almost fell. The Indians were filing off; some were already across the creek and on the meadow.

Mr. Gibbs threw himself at the old chief. "A third!" he bawled. "Just a third!" He clawed at him, and a warrior stepped over and raised his tomahawk and brought it slashing down.

Lafe screamed out. He couldn't help it. But the

tomahawk just landed flat on the side of Mr. Gibbs's head. It was a good clip—Lafe could hear the smacking sound of it plain—and he was mighty relieved that he didn't have to watch Mr. Gibbs get his skull split open. His master sank to the ground, groaning.

"Go home. Stay there. This Cherokee land. Stay home," the chief warned him. He rode off.

So there they were, while the Indians drifted leisurely away. Lafe stood quiet as a rabbit waiting to get snake-swallowed, and Tully still leaned against his tree, shaking and white-eyed. Mr. Gibbs lay on the ground, flinging around and holding his head while tears ran down his face, but Mr. Brown got up out of the dust and came and leaned over him.

"How come you to act like such a dern fool?" he asked in a disgusted voice. "If you had to go begging them red varmints for something, how come you didn't beg for my gun back? I could of shot us something to eat. *What you think we're going to do now?*"

"The old feller's right," thought Lafe wretchedly. "We're all fixing to die. We ain't got so much as a horseshoe nail left to help get us something to eat with. Here we are a million miles from nowhere, and we'll never make it back on an empty stomach."

The worst part of it was they hadn't had a proper meal for two days already. Mr. Gibbs had had them on the go so much, packing and re-dressing some of the skins and honing edges on tools, a whole bunch of steady work. He hadn't wanted to stop long enough to eat a-tall, much less fix up anything decent, so they'd got along on dried buffalo meat that was half rotten.

"Three hundred and eighty-five skins gone to ruination," Mr. Gibbs said slowly. "Ruination!"

Tully was standing up now. "You ought to of left the other day when I said let's go," he said self-righteously. "Naw, you had to be greedy and dress more skins. See what it's got you."

"If you'd helped with the work, we'd been gone a month ago," Mr. Gibbs bellowed back.

"If Tully was a half man, he'd go git my rifle-gun back from the red savages," Mr. Brown squawked, his voice cracked and furious. "He'd help out his kin what's always treated him kind."

"You shut up," hollered Tully. He swelled up like a cock turkey. "If'n you hadn't acted the fool like that, they might have left us a gun. You and Gibbs, both carrying on like that. There was no call to rile 'em up that way. If you'd kept your mouth shut, they'd have left us a knife at the least. They warn't mad till you two did what you did."

Mr. Gibbs roared out at that. "Act the fool? Act the fool? I was just trying to get my own goods back. And you'd of done the same, only you was too cowardly to stand. You was sniveling over there like a . . . like a . . ." He all but choked on his fury and bent over coughing.

Lafe wished they'd all shut up. It wasn't doing a bit of good to say what anybody should have done. If the old man had stayed in Caroliny where he belonged, he nor Tully, neither one, would be out here squabbling like this. And if Sam Birdwell had acted decent as any man should, his son Lafe would be snug at home, not caught here with these folks, not fearing slow death in the wilderness. But *that* didn't do any good to think about, he knew in reason.

"Well, you got such a notion about me, I'll leave," Tully screamed. "I'll go on off, and you can get along best you can without me. A coward won't be no help getting you back to that precious farm of yours, I'll 'low."

Mr. Gibbs rushed at him like a bull. "I'll thrash you to a pulp if'n you try it," he yelled. "You was hired out to take care of the old man, and you'll do it. You run off, and I'll track you down and kill you for sure."

Tully took a step back. His face sparkled with meanness. "You couldn't track hot butter running off," he said. "You ain't but a scabby farmer. It ain't likely you'd live long in the woods nor get home without me."

This took Mr. Gibbs back, Lafe could tell. And Tully was right. For all his hatefulness, he was a woodsman. He could trap with a handful of vines, could weave grass into a fish seine, knew just a heap of helpful things for getting along in the woods.

"I'll git home all right," promised Mr. Gibbs at last. "I been in a tight place before this. And you know it. I can get home without your help, and when I get there, I can see that you and the rest of the trifling Browns get their comeuppance."

Tully's eye fell on Lafe, and the boy thought all of a sudden he should have left till they'd quit all this. He needn't have stayed handy for everybody to take out their meanness on. "All right," Tully agreed sullenly. "I'll take care of the old man, and you won't starve neither. But I ain't going to take care of him, not that *orphan*."

"Him!" Mr. Gibbs grunted. "Ain't none of us got to worry about him."

Lafe knew what he meant by that. Tully had told. They both knew everything about him, and Mr. Gibbs figured to leave him behind. "Or they might drown me in the creek, the way they're roused up now," he thought. "It's a double wonder they didn't give me to the Injuns. I doubt I'd of been any worse off."

Well, he didn't care. He was glad they knew. He was sick to death of the lot of them, and sick of himself and of the way he'd been scared to death for most nigh a year now, jumping every time a stranger spoke to him. The way he suspicioned everybody and everything had gone on long enough. It wasn't right to have to go on living in misery for something that was no fault of his.

Tully and Mr. Gibbs could do what they dern pleased with him. He'd quit caring about anything.

Somebody behind him said, "You don't have to look after nobody, Tully. Go on off, if you're a mind to. Leave. Scat. I'll carry the rest of you back to Caroliny."

Eleven

Mr. Gibbs spun around. "McCay! Where you been?" he raged. "'How come you didn't come help us drive off them Injuns?"

Rice looked astonished. "The four of us drive off forty Cherokees?" he asked. "You must be simple. Anyway, I was a piece from here when they passed my hiding place. I seen they had your horses, and I came on back to do what I could. And it ain't much. Mostly I come back to make sure the boy and the old man get back safe to Caroliny. I ain't fixing to try to collect any skins for you or silliness such as that."

Lafe couldn't help being pleased. Rice had thought of him, had come back especially to look after him. It was a comfort to know that Rice cared what happened to him. Still and all, it didn't change matters too much. It sure didn't make it any better that Rice had turned tail and run off that time Tully was after him with a gun. If Rice was so all-fired anxious to help, how come he hadn't figured Lafe needed a friend then?

Rice had a deer. They made a fire and cooked up a heap of collops. Rice said for them all to eat hearty, they'd be leaving right away.

"You was a fool to stay here after the storm," he said. "You can see this camp from any place out on that meadow. There's Injuns all around. You were lucky you lasted this long. And if the Shawnees come on you now, they might just take your scalps, seeing that's all you got left. We got to get away fast. All manner of Injuns be coming here for their fall hunt."

Mr. Gibbs could hardly eat, he was so busy shaking his head and sighing over his losses. "Three hundred and eighty-five skins! Everything gone," he moaned. "Guns, horses—ruination!"

Rice grunted. "Seeing how the Cherokee towns were burned to the ground a few years back, you're lucky to leave a-tall," he pointed out. "They could of killed you, like their women and children got killed, and not bothered asking leave to do it."

"I never had nothing to do with that," Mr. Gibbs hastened to tell him. "They needn't take their meanness out on me. Three hundred and eighty-five skins!"

Rice didn't argue with him. It was no use, Lafe knew. Never in a hundred years would Mr. Gibbs admit the skins weren't his or that he'd done wrong to come on Injun land. He'd always claim the Cherokees stole his skins for no reason.

They left there then and traveled quickly. Mr. Brown rode Rice's horse a good part of the way, and Tully and Mr. Gibbs walked fast, not burdened by a

162

thing, with fear behind them and home in front of them. Even Tully had a home, Lafe reckoned.

Lafe was the only one who hung back. Every night he went over in his head ways to leave the others, how he would run off and hide in the woods and den up in a cave like a bear for the cold weather. Every day he figured he'd meet up with some stranger on the trail who'd hire him to go with him, and he'd go, Indians or not, he'd go and welcome the chance.

Oh, he wished he could go off with Rice. Wouldn't that be the finest kind of thing? But he wasn't easy around Rice; he didn't know yet whether to trust him. One thing was certain, Rice hadn't offered to take Lafe anywhere. The young hunter hardly spoke to him, and not much to the others either. He just went along his own way, as he used to do.

It wasn't till they'd been traveling several days that Rice seemed to take notice that Lafe was really there. Lafe was lagging. Somehow he never seemed able to keep up with the others, and the closer they got to Carolina, the more he was apt to fall behind. He didn't yearn for Tully's company, anyway, not Mr. Gibbs's either, for that matter.

That day Rice waited for him to catch up and fell

in step beside him. "You sick or something?" he wanted to know. "You trailing along here looking like a calf with the molligrubbles."

Lafe barely looked up. He was carrying a stick, and he swung it at a half-opened milkweed pod, sending a puff of feathery seeds upward. "Naw, I ain't sick," he answered at last. "I just don't hanker to be with folks, is all."

Rice smiled. "All right, then, I'll leave you be," he told him, but Lafe reached out and grabbed him. "Wait, Rice," he cried. "Tell me something. I reckon you don't have to say, but I been wondering. I been wondering a long time now." He took a deep breath. "How come you to run off that time Tully tried to get Mr. Brown to shoot you? Back there at the camp? And I hollered, and you never come, just lit out runnin'."

Rice's face went hard as iron, and for a minute he didn't speak. Finally he said, "When you yelled, I seen how it was and what Tully had it in mind to do. I ain't the best person alive, I don't reckon, and I got a temper like you ain't never seen the likes of. I run, I tell you; I left there like a busted-out case of the measles. I knew if I crossed that creek, I'd kill

Tully for sure. I run away afore I could kill him and maybe Old Man Brown, too, for I was mad enough to tear up trees. I . . ."

Rice broke off. He was telling the truth, Lafe knew. And he could almost see how it was. Anyway, Rice hadn't deserted him, not all the way. He'd been hanging around the camp all the time; he'd just never come where they could see him.

They walked on, and Lafe pondered, and finally he made up his mind. "Rice," he said, "get me some deer meat and a knife or hatchet or something and show me a trail where I can go off some place by myself."

Rice stared at him. "What in thunderation *does* ail you?" he asked. "What makes you think you could get along by yourself out in the woods, without no gun and nobody to help you. And how come you want to? What would your folks think? Ain't you got nobody to go back to?"

Lafe grimaced as though he'd bitten one of the green persimmons lying in the trail. "I ain't got no folks," he muttered. "Leastways, not hardly, I ain't. And that's how come I don't want to go back. I ain't just Lafe Birdwell. I'm Sam Birdwell's son. I reckon you've heard of him, how he give the Injuns the guns out of his trading store and sent 'em rampaging over the countryside . . ."

His voice faltered, and he was quiet, walking slowly and watching his moccasins go in and out, in and out beneath him, as his feet moved listlessly along.

For a while Rice didn't say one thing. They went through a beech forest and scared up a huge flock of pigeons. After a spell, he spoke. "Naw, I ain't heard the tale. Do ye know it to be true? Have you heard, for a fact?"

Lafe shook his head. "It don't make no difference, folks think it's true. I been up and down the country-side trying to get away from all the talk, but somehow they always find out about me. Then they're just as hateful as if it was true."

"Well, let 'em be," Rice replied, and his voice was grim. "No matter what folks do to you, it can't be no worse than running and hiding all the time. If'n I was you, I'd go on back. Stand up to their meanness. That way you got something to fight back against. It ain't like suspicioning everybody that comes along. It ain't like knowing what you know and forever waiting for somebody else to find out."

He clamped his jaws together suddenly and strode away along the path up ahead of Lafe. The boy stood still a minute, looking after him. Rice didn't know how it was. He'd never had to worry about such things and never would, most likely.

And yet in a way Rice was right, for Lafe Birdwell was about as tired of waiting for somebody to accuse him of being a traitor as he ever hoped to be of anything.

A week later Mr. Gibbs whooped out, "Yonder it is! Yonder's the Trading Ford of the Yadkin. We're well nigh home."

A moment later they were standing on the bank of the river, staring across at the island and beyond to where the path went up the other shore. "We be here all right," agreed Rice. "Salisbury ain't too far off. Git the old feller off my horse."

Mr. Gibbs looked astonished. "How come?" he asked. "Ain't you going on with us?"

Rice shook his head. "Naw, we go different ways from here on in," he answered softly. "A heap different ways, I reckon. I'm staying here a couple days, and then I'll head on north toward Virginny."

"Well, it's your doings." Mr. Gibbs shrugged. "We don't need your gun no more. It's pretty settled across the river. Come on, boys." He rushed down the bank and splashed through the shallow water below the island.

Mr. Gibbs looked his old self again. Lafe guessed he'd figured out some new scheme to make back the money he lost on this hunting journey. For a moment he watched the water rise up and cover more and more of Mr. Gibbs's patched leather breeches, the ones he always claimed had belonged to his old pa. They'd been patched so much, in some places patch on top of patch, that Lafe doubted any of Mr. Gibbs's pa's breeches was left.

Tully led the old man across, and Lafe followed along behind them—out of pure habit, he reckoned —and stopped with the water around his knees to wave to Rice. But the young hunter was upstream hobbling his horse among the cane. Lafe went on, and at the far shore he turned again. Rice McCay stood at the water's edge, looking after them. Lafe raised a hand. He would have liked to say good-by proper and offer his thanks for all Rice had done, but he hadn't been able to, couldn't somehow.

168

Rice waved once, then Lafe turned and tagged along with the others. What else could he do? Uncle George lived south of Salisbury, a far piece on beyond Gibbs's farm. He would try to get Mr. Gibbs to pay him; then he'd go on and see if Uncle George was willing to take him in for the winter.

He stopped to watch a little wood mouse nibbling at a shed deer antler, then had to run to catch up with the others. Mr. Gibbs had taken up singing hymns again, and Mr. Brown was babbling a mile a minute, asking Tully where they were now, every few steps.

Once Lafe found a piece of odd-shaped chalky rock in the path. He picked it up, and at the first boulder he came to, he stopped to print his initials. The B was hard to do, as was the R he drew down below his own letters. LB and RM. Suddenly he threw down the chalk. What was he doing, lalling away his time here? He had to get on.

He ran and ran, but he had fallen so far behind he'd lost the others. Even from a rise he couldn't see them on the path. For one long moment he stood staring ahead, wondering why he had wanted to catch up with those three, anyway. He turned around quick and flew back the way he'd come.

When he reached the Yadkin, he could see Rice sitting by a little fire he'd made downstream a way. He waded across, and the young hunter watched him come without getting up or even calling out a greeting. He was boiling sassafras tea, and it smelled good to Lafe, climbing up the slope to stand beside him.

"Now what you doing back here, bonehead?" Rice asked coldly.

"Rice, Rice," Lafe pleaded. "Don't go off to Virginny. Let's you and me go off together in the woods and hunt the winter long. Mr. Gibbs don't aim to pay me no wage anyhow, I know he don't, the things he's said lately since he lost them skins and all. I ain't got no reason to go back. Me and you could go off, just us, and not have to see any of the folks around Salisbury or them up in Virginny either, not ever again. Please, Rice."

The hunter stirred the tea. "It wouldn't do you no good," he said dully. "You'd be just as bad off as ever. You'd be waiting all the time for somebody to come along and haul you back. You'd get where you thought I was the one going to do it. And maybe I would. I got a temper. If'n I got mad at you, I might recollect you was a traitor's son and just whonk you a good one over the head. Or sell you off to the Injuns. Or anything."

Lafe hunkered by the fire. "You wouldn't, Rice, would you?" he asked, only he asked the words inside his head. He didn't say them aloud. He felt kind of sick, and there was a cold lump in his chest no fire could ever warm, he didn't reckon.

Rice poured out the tea into two horns. "Let me tell you a story," he said. "Once there was a feller I knew, and he was young and hot-headed. He liked horses, see, and there was a horse he wanted to buy the worst way. He kept on trying to get the money, and he worked and traded and did every living thing he knew how. Finally he sold his gun and his dog and the shirt off his back, well-nigh, till he had the money in his hand. He went to the horse's owner and said, 'Here I am with the price, let me have the horse,' and the man told him, 'I done raised the price five pounds.' Well, like I said, that young feller was hot-headed. He jumped on the man, and they had such a wrangle as you never saw. And when it was over, the man was a-laying there dead."

Folks were always fighting over something, but most generally over horses up in Virginia, Lafe remembered. He didn't reckon he'd be willing to fight over anything—well, maybe a rifle, a long, slim, handsome one like Rice owned. That, now, might be worth a fight.

"The young 'un—he was big but wasn't much older than you—he lit out. He run and run, and he run and run, and he's running to this day. I've heared him say many a time he wished he hadn't run. How he wished he'd stayed and faced up to things!"

A thunder pumper flew up from the island and flapped off down the river, its cry of "pump-er-lunk" so loud and sudden that Lafe dropped his horn.

Rice poured him some more tea and went on. "No-body's ever come after that feller. But there ain't a day goes by, he don't wish he had the guts to take what was coming to him, however bad. It's like he says, you can get away with anything, like he got away with murder. But somehow you can't get away with running off; you got to think about it again every

172

morning when you wake up. It goes with you wherever you go."

Lafe looked stubborn. "That feller done a wrong thing, and I didn't," he said. "It ain't like that with me."

"Yes, it is, too," spoke Rice. "You're hiding just as much as he is. I seen how everything Tully said made you shiver. If the truth had been out in the open, you wouldn't have worried."

Lafe reckoned maybe that was right. He'd got awful tired of watching everything he did and said and waiting for something terrible to happen. Still, he'd got awful tired of folks being mean to him, too.

"Well, I could go back next year, it might be," he said uncertainly. "Couldn't we go off in the woods now and then maybe next spring come back to the settlements?"

Rice stood up and emptied the last of his tea into the fire. "Naw," he answered. "We couldn't, for you know that young feller, the one that done the murder? Well, he's going back home and give hisself up. I know, on account of I'm him."

Twelve

Lafe bent over to chop at the root of a sapling, and something queer came over him. He stayed that way, his ax in his hand and his back crooked, feeling like the world didn't quite make sense and not able to figure out just what it was. As if he'd put his nose down in the dark red bloom of a sweet shrub and smelled, not the tangy, fruity smell he'd expected,

174

but the rotten stink of skunk cabbage. Of a sudden, what had made things so turned around?

Then he knew. Bending over like that, slicing at the tree—it had put him in mind of the hunting camp, back there at the edge of that big meadow, and how he'd cleared the path down to the spring. For just that little spell he had been far away, still in the wild, remote lands of the Cherokees and not here at Uncle George's.

He couldn't think of two more different places, for a fact. There, in the heat of August, surrounded by men and wet skins and the gear of hunting, in that flat rolling country, wasn't a thing like here among the little ridges of Rowan County. Here it was a spring day, cool and new, full of the freshness of April and the songs of birds. Even here in the deadening, green things pushed up from the dirt through the wood chips. The blue hills rimmed the sky, and down their sides trickled the goldy stream of young poplar groves, and in their hollows the dogwood blossoms had taken the place of sarvis berry and was even now waiting to shatter.

Lafe sighed. This was pleasant country. The work he did for Uncle George was hard, but not so hard that he couldn't stand it. Still, he'd rather be off to the west, hunting and looking about at the sights. It had been an uncertain life from day to day, but he'd got to like the dangers and the loneliness. Now in truth, he felt bound and stifled on a farm. Closed in, sort of. From the top of the next rise, you could see the smoke of three different cabins, and it made Lafe uneasy. It was settling up too fast.

He promised himself he would get a rifle of his own and a horse and leave. He knew in reason he could, maybe not this year, but soon. Then he'd ride away from here and out into the wilderness, and this time it would be even better, without Mr. Brown to hang to his shirttails, without Tully's meanness and Mr. Gibbs's hard-handedness and blows.

But he hoped he could take somebody along when the time came. A body liked a little company to share his finds and his adventures with. Rice, now, he'd be the best kind of company on a hunt, the very best. But Rice . . . Lafe shivered. Better to be working on a farm in the sunshine, better to be a cobbler's apprentice in the heart of some city, than to be shut up in a jail, moldering the days away with a big M branded on your cheek. Or worse yet, hanged by the high sheriff's hand and left dead from a crossbeam.

He began to hack away with his ax, stripping the limbs off a dead tree. He'd cleared most of this new ground his very own self and made a good job of it. Uncle George hadn't had any call to regret taking him back when the hunt was over.

Lafe grinned a little to himself. He remembered the way it had been when he got back and turned up at Uncle George's once again. Uncle George wasn't close-fisted like Mr. Gibbs, but he was thrifty enough. He hadn't wanted to turn Lafe from his door, not a good, big, able-bodied boy, eleven years old and a hard worker, who could turn his hand to most anything and do it well.

At the same time he knew well enough that Lafe was the traitor's son. Many of the neighbors might think shame of him for sheltering such a lad, for Lafe had been right. The news had dogged him right to Uncle George's door, and everybody for miles around had had the story.

Uncle George near about split in two, trying to make up his mind. But he'd made it up at last. "You can stay," he said finally. "Folks'll find something else to talk about soon."

"He was sure right," Lafe said aloud, cutting a big wedge out of a hickory on the side he aimed for it to fall toward. He moved around to the other half of the trunk and made a smaller cut. Giving the swaying tree a push with his hand, he leaped away before the hickory crashed.

"And Rice had been right, too," he thought, "right about standing up to folks's meanness." It had been hard, oh, it had been mortal hard! He recalled right this minute the sour taste of anger that had welled up in his throat when some folks spit at him and some cursed him. There was even a man who clean to this day wouldn't lend Uncle George an adze or trade him a setting of eggs because he'd sheltered the traitor's son. Lafe was grateful to Uncle George.

And he remembered to the day the time it came over him that Uncle George didn't have a thing to do with traitors—and that he didn't neither. He was his own man, Lafe Birdwell, who could plow as straight a furrow or chop a log as clean as any man's son. All the talk in the world couldn't change that, and that was what mattered.

From then on he had minded folks's spiteful ways less and less. He held his head high and went about his business the best way he knew how. Soon folks talked about the King's Proclamation Line along the top of the Blue Ridge and how all land beyond belonged to the Indians, and about how the lightning had lasted all winter and struck only walnut trees. And about how Farrar Beane had died of a snake bite that went right through his thick boots.

Some forgot that Lafe had a stain on his name; and some remembered but were willing to admit he wasn't responsible for his father's crime; and some even said they'd heard that Sam Birdwell had died of a fever among the Indians, and that was when the savages stole the guns.

Lafe didn't suppose things had worked out quite so well for Rice. He doubted folks ever forgave a murderer. Lafe had been back in Rowan County six months now, and not a day went by he didn't think of the young hunter and remind himself that Rice had gone fearlessly back to much worse things than Lafe had had to face.

He shouldered his ax and went over and took a deep drink of the milk from the gourd he'd left in the roots of a big oak. He gazed upward into the branches. The little pinky leaves were spreading out every day, and he'd have to quit this chopping soon and help Uncle George with the planting.

A robin whistled from the top of the tree. And he could hear Uncle George's cows bawling and, way beyond that, the ring of Amos Bandy's ax. "Too many folks too close," Lafe thought. And sure enough, here came horse's hoofs. It was the third person who'd ridden by this distant field in the past week.

Lafe turned away and went to work trimming the trees felled that morning. He heard the horse slow down to a walk and then stop, but he kept his back to the rider. It wouldn't be anybody he knew, likely. He kept chopping; he hoped to get through with this before he went to the cabin for the midday meal.

"Hey, you!" the rider called out gruffly. "Ain't you got no manners? I done yelled twice already at you. Can't you speak friendly to a lost stranger?"

Lafe never looked around. "I ain't feeling friendly," he thought, but instead he said shortly, "Howdy. Fine day."

"Is that all you got to say?" the newcomer said. "You're 'bout the stupidest boy I've run across."

Lafe reckoned he might be stupid, but he wasn't

lost. The ax struck a dead limb with an echoing chonk.

"Don't reckon it'd do any good to ask you where Sam Birdwell's son lives," the stranger went on.

Lafe jumped. Well, he was through with all that. Let the newcomer say what he liked. Lafe Birdwell was still a master chopper. He swung and hit a knot, and his hands tingled. He threw down the ax and turned around, squinting in the sunlight. The rider wasn't anybody he knew, as far as he could tell in the glare.

"You couldn't be the Birdwell boy, I 'low," the man called. "I'd know him anywhere. They say he's eat so much buffalo meat, he's done grown a hump. I hear he's so tough the sunshine is scared to get near him, so fierce he fought a hurricane with one hand tied behind him and gave the hurricane the first bite." The man laughed out.

It couldn't be! Lafe was running toward the rider. "Rice," he yelled. "Oh, Rice!"

Paler, thinner, maybe, but still Rice. Lafe stopped by the horse and stretched up to put a hand on Rice's arm. "What you doing here?" He gulped. "Is any-

181

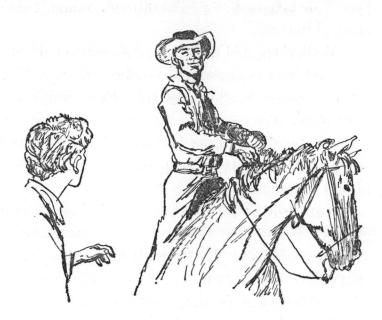

body seen you? When did you break out of jail? Do you aim to hide out around here? I know a dandy place. They'll never find you."

He knew Rice had escaped, for he was wearing a hat to hide his face. Lafe had never known him to wear a head covering of any kind. His queue was cut off, and he'd spoken out in that gruff voice. He was hiding, no doubt of it.

Rice slid down off his horse. "Ain't I done told

you?" he asked quietly. "I'm through hiding. I ain't run off from nothing."

"Well, then, h-how come . . ." stammered Lafe.

"I got back home, and about the first body I laid eyes on was that feller I had the fight with," Rice explained. "He wasn't dead. I won't say I done him any good with the beating I give him, but anyway I didn't kill him. He was lucky, but I was luckier. And I ain't running ever again."

It was true. The closed door behind Rice's eyes was gone. Lafe was glad with all his heart, but it made Rice look a little different. Lafe was almost shy of him until he smiled.

"You getting on all right?" Rice asked.

"Fine," Lafe answered. "It ain't bad here no more. It's just, well, I sort of lost my taste for farming out yonder in the woods, I reckon. I aim to go hunting again some day."

"Go with me," Rice said. "Come summer, I mean to go west, maybe as far as the Mississippi River. Hunting and exploring. I could use a young feller to go along with me."

Lafe could hardly believe his ears. It didn't seem possible that something he'd hankered for so hard could be happening to him in the best way he could imagine. He put out his hand and touched the horse. "Would it be all right for me to go, reckon?" he asked suddenly. "I'd be running away again, seems like."

"Would you?" asked Rice.

Lafe pondered. And he saw suddenly that it wouldn't because he didn't care who knew or didn't know. And what folks thought about Sam Birdwell couldn't change Lafe Birdwell a mite. It wouldn't change the way he could scrape a hide or build a fire. It wouldn't change the way he meant to learn to shoot game.

He grinned, a grin a mile wide, it felt like. "Reckon I wouldn't be," he said triumphantly. "When you figure we'll be leaving?"